Murder at the Shrimp Festival

A Lt. Maggie Watson Murder Mystery

Murder at the Shrimp Festival

Lt. Maggie Watson Murder Mystery

MW Burdette

Printed in the United States of America. For information, contact Amazon.com at www.amazon.com.

ISBN-13: 9798801421483

Original Publication Date: 2022. Published in the United States of America by Amazon.com.

For Martha

CONTENTS

Prologue

PART I: Shrimp is King

Shrimp, Shrimp, Shrimp
Panic at the Beach
Official Business
Exhaustion
A Coordinated Effort
Punishment
Reading the Tea Leaves
A Persecuted Mind
Larry Pennington's Profile
Running the Gauntlet

PART II: The Fear of the Unknown

Exposing the Perp's Identity
Details, Details
Digging Deeper
Deductive Reasoning
Time for Another Dose
Cold Feet
All Bets are Off
Playing the Long Game

Epilogue

Prologue

There are a few people in this world who either can't eat shrimp, because of an allergic reaction to shellfish, or because they have religious objections to eating the scavengers of the seas, but for the most part, *everyone* else loves shrimp. To my knowledge, there has not been a national poll taken as to who loves shrimp and who do not. They are just wonderful little creatures to watch, and luscious to eat when boiled, fried, sauteed, or cooked in any kind of stew or gumbo. If you were just arriving along the Gulf Coast of the Southern United States, that land bordering the southeastern most area of South Florida to the southwestern most area of Texas, and your home planet was Mars, or somewhere else in the galaxy, you would benefit from Wikipedia's definition of a shrimp.

Shrimp are decapod crustaceans with elongated bodies and a primarily swimming mode of locomotion – most commonly Caridea and Dendrobranchiata. More narrow definitions may be restricted to Caridea, to smaller species of either group or to only the marine species. Under a broader definition, shrimp may be synonymous with prawn, covering stalk-eyed swimming crustaceans with long, narrow muscular tails (abdomens), long whiskers (antennae), and slender legs. Any small crustacean which resembles a shrimp tends to be called one. They swim forward by paddling with swimmerets on the underside of their abdomens, although their escape response is typically repeated flicks with the tail driving them backwards very quickly. Crabs and lobsters have strong walking legs, whereas shrimp have thin, fragile legs which they use primarily for perching

Shrimp are widespread and abundant. There are thousands of species adapted to a wide range of habitats. They can be found feeding near the seafloor on most coasts and estuaries, as well as in rivers and lakes. To escape predators, some species flip off the seafloor and dive into the sediment. They usually live from one to seven years. Shrimp are often solitary, though they can form large schools during the spawning season.

Shrimp play important roles in the food chain and are an important food source for larger animals ranging from fish to whales. The muscular tails of many shrimps are edible to humans, and they are widely caught and farmed for human consumption. Commercial shrimp species support an industry worth 50 billion dollars a year, and in 2010 the total commercial production of shrimp was nearly 7 million tons. Shrimp farming became more prevalent during the 1980s, particularly in China, and by 2007 the harvest from shrimp farms exceeded the capture of wild shrimp.

Whew! More than anyone ever wanted, or needed, to know about the little scavengers of the sea! What we really need to know as a general population is that shellfish allergies can be brutal, and at times, fatal. Most people who have been diagnosed as being allergic to shellfish, such as shrimp, crabs, lobsters, and most other crustaceans, keep medication on hand to act as a neutralizing effect if they come contact with shellfish. Mild reactions are generally limited to hives, itching, swelling of lips, face, tongue, and throat. According to physicians who have diagnosed and treated most people for shellfish allergies tell us that the reaction can be dangerous and life threatening, and that having an Epinephrine Auto-Injector readily available is a must for those with extreme reactions to shellfish consumption.

Before you put all shellfish on your "Do not consume" list, you should know that only about 2% of all Americans have any allergic reaction to shellfish. Some of those can eat one kind of shellfish, but they are ill-advised to eat another kind unless they have been tested by their allergist and know that they probably will not have a radical reaction to the oysters, scallops, and similar seafood.

Why all the concern and breast-beating about the little scavengers of the sea? Why is it important to know if you can consume them, assuming you want to do that? It's very simple. They are scrumptious little things! In fact, they are so good that many areas of the United States, and all around the world, have shrimp festivals, where the little crustaceans are considered King of the Festival! Every city that hosts a seafood festival believes that their festival is the best! While no one can truly judge "The best" seafood festival objectively, one of the most attended and appreciated by local residents and visitors alike is the one held every fall in Gulf Shores, Alabama. The event even bears the name National Shrimp Festival, and for very good reasons. An average of 225,000 people visit every year, there are 40 food booths, arts and crafts, and every kind of prepared shrimp known to man. And, if those weren't reasons enough to declare Gulf Shores the Shrimp Festival of the World, the revenue to the city of Gulf Shores is always in excess of five million dollars. That's a lot of shrimp.

When several visitors to the shrimp festival began checking themselves into the South Baldwin Medical Center for food poisoning just two days into the festivities, the organizers of the festival, as well as the city of Gulf Shores, became concerned that there may be more than just too much sun, beer, and fried food making their visitors ill. When two of those who got sick died after a day of food sickness symptoms, it was time to call in the best detective agency in the state to help stop the spread of whatever was out to destroy the integrity of the National Shrimp Festival.

PART I: Shrimp is King

Chapter 1

Shrimp, Shrimp, Shrimp!

Who doesn't love shrimp? Of all the seafood consumed in the United States annually, shrimp makes up almost 50% of the volume of fish served, and it is not surprising. Shrimp is easy to clean, cook, and eat. Jonathan and Maggie were introducing Maria and Jo-Ellen to the National Shrimp Festival for their first time since they had just arrived in Gulf Shores after the Shrimp Festival last year.

"What's all the fuss about?" Maria asked innocently.

"Maria, Maria, Maria!" Jonathan said with extra stress on the third time he called her name. "The National Shrimp Festival is to Gulf Shores as the Boston Red Socks are to Boston; they're the Statue of Liberty in D.C.; the Empire State Building in Manhattan; and the Rotunda in Washington all rolled into one big celebration!" Maria eyed Jonathan skeptically, then made a resounding statement.

"What's so great about those places?" Maggie and Jo-Ellen almost fell down laughing. Jo-Ellen thought if Jonathan had compared the festival to the Library of Congress or the New York Public Library for the Arts, he might have connected with her. Maria liked seafood, and she liked shrimp. She also liked lamb, beef, chicken, and pork. To Maria, it was all just food. Shrimp was good, but so was porkchops. She couldn't understand the significance of the shrimp festival in their everyday lives.

"Jonathan, Maria is a practical girl. There are very few things that she really craves when it comes to food, and shrimp is just one more of the things she can take or leave," Jo-Ellen said as she stoked Maria's long black hair.

"Now you really have my curiosity up," Jonathan teased. "So, what is the only food you really couldn't live without, Maria?" She thought a minute then gave an answer that Jonathan had difficulty believing.

"Chocolate bon-bons," Maria said. "I really like Chocolate bon-bons more than anything in the world." Jonathan just looked at her like she had two heads, but he wisely dropped the subject. Maggie decided that she would step in and change the subject to a more agreeable conversation.

"We should have brought Molly to the festival. Lots of people have their dogs here, and she would simply love it. Of course, at her age, the heat might be too much for her."

"Jonathan, what does one do at a shrimp festival except eat shrimp?" Jo-Ellen asked.

"There's lots of fun things to do, like potato sack races, horseshoes, cow-patty throwing, and face painting. It will be fun for all!"

"Cow patty throwing?" Maggie asked, shrinking back as if Jonathan had said he had a contagious disease.

"Not real cow patties, Maggie. Just some leather pouches that resemble cow patties."

"What's the purpose of cow patty throwing?"

"According to some of the old-timers, the original contest used real cow chips, and the person who could throw it the farthest won a prize."

"Why in the world would someone create such a dumb contest?" Jo-Ellen asked.

"Jo-Ellen, we are all from the city, and there were many things available for us to do in Rowlette, New York, and Chicago. In the country, on a farm, there aren't many things to entertain people. Back in the 1920s and 1930s, there was no television, few radios, and farmers worked seven days a week. Cows had to be milked, the hay had to be cut and put in the barn, chickens had to be fed, eggs had to be gathered twice a day, and wood had to be chopped for fireplaces. There were no electric heaters or gas furnaces back then—only firewood or coal to burn for heating and cooking.

Everyone got up with the chickens, because someone had to feed them and gather the eggs. Cows have to be milked every day, and there was butter to be churned, cheese to be made, and livestock to be fed and put out to pasture. A man was blessed when he had sons because they could work much more efficiently than daughters. Life on a farm out in the country away from civilization was difficult, and there were very few distractions that satisfied the farmer and his kids other than using what was available to entertain themselves. Cow chip throwing was free and a diversion from their everyday hard lives."

"Since you are our resident historian," Maggie teased, "tell us the origin of the cow chip toss." Maggie watched Maria and Jo-Ellen as Jonathan began speaking authoritatively about the history of cow chip tossing in America.

"How old do you think cow chip throwing is?" Jonathan asked no one in particular.

"Probably a couple of hundred years old, I would guess," Maggie answered.

"Historians date official townships in Colonial America competing in cow chip throwing dating back to the 17th century, with the town crier announcing the event from the town square prior to the games beginning. However, some anthropologists believe that cow chips contests date back over 100,000 years, with skilled throwers bringing down small game and birds by accurately aiming the hard cow manure at their targets and striking them hard enough to either kill them or stun them so they could be captured and killed for food." Maggie raised an eyebrow, indicating that she wasn't too sure about Jonathan's facts at that point.

"Now I guess you are going to tell us about some famous people who were known for cow chip throwing, right?" Jo-Ellen challenged him.

"For your information and edification, cow chip tossing was originally one of the events in the Greek Olympics."

"Jonathan, you're kidding, aren't you?" Maria said.

"According to legend, after Scatos of Athens was crowned the first winner of the cow chip competition in the games in 472 BC, the event was removed from the competition in the year 468 BC. No one ever said why the event was removed but it was the last time it was ever mentioned by Greek historians."

"You're making all that up to entertain us," Jo-Ellen began to laugh.

"No, I'm not," Jonathan insisted. "Do you know that eventually cow chip tossing was considered a crime in Ancient Rome, and do you have any idea why that might be?" This was getting deep, or at least Maggie thought so, but she took the bait.

"No, Jonathan, but I'll bet you can tell us."

"According to Roman historians, an errant cow chip missed its mark and landed in Nero's bathtub. He immediately made it a capital crime if someone was caught throwing cow chips!" Maggie and Jo-Ellen began to laugh so hard that they were actually shedding tears. Maria was just shaking her head in disbelief, but Jonathan would not admit that any of his research was farfetched or exaggerated.

"And for that reason alone, we should all enjoy the National Shrimp Festival!" When Jonathan finished speaking, Jo-Ellen and Maggie began to clap loudly, whistle, and generally make fools of themselves. "You laugh now, one day if you ever need survival training, the cow patty toss might just save your life."

"Oh, Jonathan, you slay me!" Maggie pulled him down to her face and gave him a big kiss on the mouth. "Even if you weren't a great lover in bed and worth more money than anyone I know, I would still love you for your imagination!" Now, Jo-Ellen, Maria, and Maggie were all laughing at the overall situation. Jonathan told them that it was time to find a good shrimp vendor and get some lunch.

“There’s a place,” Maggie said and indicated a makeshift bar with stools and umbrellas to shield the patrons from the overbearing heat being generated by the sun and its reflection by the white sand. The name on the temporary shrimp stand was Hot to Trot Shrimp and Fixins.

“It looks as good as any other place around here,” Jonathan said. “Let’s get some shrimp, beer, and fixins, and begin enjoying this annual feast of the sea!”

“You are so dramatic,” Maggie said. She enjoyed Jonathan’s antics, but sometimes he was a lot to digest. However, Maggie was getting hungry, and Jonathan was the only one of them with money on his person, so she would go along to get along, especially if Jonathan was buying lunch. They let Jonathan decide what they would eat, with each of them ordering their own preference to drink with the shrimp feast. Maggie had a beer, Jo-Ellen and Maria had white wine, and Jonathan got himself two beers to start. He didn’t want to run out of something to wash down the shrimp with halfway through his meal. When he returned to the table with the food, he had multiple containers of shrimp.

“What have we here?” Maggie asked.

“Shrimp, my love. Beautiful, wonderful shrimp!” he boasted.

"But what kind of shrimp?" Maggie persisted.

"Well, let's analyze this situation," Jonathan said. "In this container we have fried popcorn shrimp; in container two, we have sauteed jumbo shrimp in drawn garlic butter; in container three, we have barbecued shrimp with teriyaki sauce; and in container four, we have coconut shrimp, gently pan fried in island spices." Maggie had never seen so much cooked shrimp in one setting in all her life.

"How much shrimp did you order?" Maggie asked.

"A pound of shrimp each of these four delicious recipes," he said. Jonathan appeared to be lusting over the little creatures just looking for a place to dive into the meal. "Oh, I almost forgot." He disappeared from the table momentarily and returned with two bread baskets full of hushpuppies and French fries.

"Jonathan, do you really think you and three women with good manners will be able to eat all of this food at one seating?"

"I really never considered it one way or the other, but shrimp warms up nicely in the microwave!" he said with a huge grin. "Ok, girls. Dig in!"

While they did their best to consume all of the shrimp, hushpuppies, and French fries, it was obvious that there would be leftovers. Jonathan went back to the serving counter and got some doggy boxes to take the uneaten food home with them. It was now getting late in the afternoon, the sun was unbearably hot, and Maggie thought that they all had had enough exposure to the sun's rays for the day, so she suggested that they go home and rest the remaining part of the day. They all agreed, and in a matter of minutes they were walking back to their condominium which was just a few hundred feet from the main event. It was convenient that all four of them lived in the Crown Victoria Condominium, although Jo-Ellen and Maria lived on the eighth floor, while Jonathan and Maggie owned the entire eighteenth floor of the complex. Jonathan had promised Maggie if she would move to Gulf Shores with him and retire from the Rowlette Police Department in Illinois that he would build her a mansion on the beach. And he was true to his word.

Jo-Ellen and Maria gave Jonathan and Maggie a hug, got on one of the elevators, and were whisked away upward to their unit. Jonathan and Maggie had a dedicated elevator which made only one stop in the building, and that was when it opened into the foyer of their condominium suite that consisted of more than 25,000 square feet of unimaginable elegance overlooking the Gulf of

Mexico some 180 feet above the bustling crowd of tourists below. Jonathan had the office and their private suite designed as part of the construction project of the building. He also owned Jo-Ellen's and Maria's unit, and he allowed them to live there as part of their compensation package to come to work at M&J Investigations. Jonathan really was rich, and money was only a vehicle for him to do the things he wanted to do to help Maggie ease into a slower lifestyle, and to fund their non-profit detective agency. It was designed to help and aid small government police departments and municipalities to solve crimes they otherwise would not have the resources to tackle under normal circumstances. As they rode the elevator up to their safe nest in the sky, Maggie snuggled up against him.

"You know that I really love you, don't you Jonathan?" He loved it when she got mellow and let her hair down. He always let her set the pace of their intimate moments, and she could be as hotblooded as one dancers at the nightclubs on the beach. He never pushed her, but he always was able to stay engaged until she had had her fill of him. They weren't married, and seemed hardly engaged to one another, but when Maggie let down her hair, she really let down her hair.

As soon as the elevator opened into their unit, Maggie began shedding her clothes on the way to their oversized Jacuzzi. In a flash the tub was filling up with water with a naked Maggie sitting in the middle of the tub beckoning for Jonathan to join her. She never had to ask him twice to join her in the Jacuzzi, the shower, or the bed. On his way to the Jacuzzi, Jonathan stopped by the kitchen, grabbed a bottle of champagne with two glasses, and popped the cork as he approached the water where his beloved waited for him. He had slipped out of his clothes as well, and Maggie could see that Jonathan was ready for action.

"Do you come here often?" she cooed.

"Not often enough," he said, nuzzling her neck. They drank champagne, played in the bubbling Jacuzzi, and eventually wound up in the bed. After some serous lovemaking, they both fell asleep. Two hours later they were awakened by Molly barking in her room down the hall. Jonathan looked at the clock on the nightstand and realized that they had slept four hours without as much as turning over in the bed. It was 8:00 PM, and they had a very hungry little Westie complaining about not having been fed on time. Maggie started to get up and take care of Molly's food, but Jonathan convinced her that he would get the job done right. It didn't take much to convince Maggie to roll over and go back to sleep. Within twenty minutes of waking, Molly had been fed, and Jonathan let her get in the bed between he and Maggie to pacify her being so upset. Thinking back on the day, it had been a wonderful, almost perfect day. As Jonathan slipped back into slumberland, he wondered if tomorrow would be as perfect.

Chapter 2

Panic at the Beach

There have many jokes made about not screaming out the word “fire” at the movie theatre, but there as just about as much panic created on the beach when someone screams “shark.” Neither of these words was recommended to be shouted in a crowd, even if there were a fire or a shark endangering the people’s lives. When people panic, people usually die. Put 150 people in close quarters in a movie theatre, and when the movie is over and everyone is leaving at the same time, it is clear that if those same people were running or screaming to try to get to the exits all at the same time, tragedy would be the end result more times than not. Now imagine 1700 times as many people than were in that theatre in relatively close quarters on a public beach panicking because of the fear of the unknown. A shark sighting could start a stampede which could injure or kill hundreds of vacationers. Any direct threat to the lives of those enjoying themselves could immediately turn a happy and jolly crowd into a frenzied moving mass of manhood, injuring or killing younger and weaker people in their rush to leave the area. Jonathan and Maggie were about to be introduced to something worse than the threat of a shark at the shrimp festival, and when their telephones rang the third morning of the shrimp festival, uncontrollable forces were on the verge of breaking loose and causing the kind of chaos just discussed.

"Jonathan, answer your phone," Maggie complained as she covered her head back up with the blanket. The light was streaming into their private quarters, so Jonathan knew it was later than they normally rose on a workday. He looked at the clock by the bed, picked up his chirping cell phone, and answered sleepily.

"Hello. Who's calling?" He wasn't unfriendly, but he wasn't Mr. Sunshine, either.

"Is this Jonathan Pembroke?"

"It is. Who are you?"

"The Jonathan Pembroke of the M&J Detective Agency?"

"The one and only. Now that you know who I am, why don't you tell me who you are before I hang up this phone."

"Oh, no. Please don't hang up. I need to speak to you right away," the voice droned on.

"I'm giving you exactly ten seconds to tell me who you are and why you're calling me." Jonathan began to count backwards from the number ten.

“My name is Ferdinand Scott, and I’m the artistic director of the National Shrimp Festival. You’ve probably never heard of me, but I’m sure you’ve heard of the shrimp festival,” Ferdinand said. “You can call me Scott.”

“OK, Scott. How may I help you today? I’m just waking up after a big day at your festival, and it may take me a minute to get my mind in gear. Tell me why you called my agency, and I’ll tell you if I think we can help you.”

“Oh, you must help us,” Scott persisted. “We are doomed without your help!” Even though Jonathan was not fully awake, this guy seemed over the top in his anxiety.

“Scott, just start from the beginning and tell me why you’re so upset, and why you think that we may be able to help you with whatever problem you may have.” It was difficult for Jonathan to form intelligent sentences when awakened from a deep sleep, but he was trying his hardest to make sense.

“I’m assuming you have not seen the local morning news channel.”

“No, but I’ll turn it on and get caught up with whatever is bothering you.”

“It won’t help that much, because they have their facts wrong. They are blowing the deaths at the festival all out of proportion.” Maggie was still sleeping, so Jonathan slipped out of bed, quietly made his way into the office, and thought that Jo-Ellen and Maria be there soon because the clock on the wall read 7:45 AM. Then Jonathan remembered that it was Sunday, and that the office was closed today. He plopped down on the sofa in their elaborate waiting room in the office and turned on the big-screen television mounted on the opposite wall from where he was sitting. Across the bottom of the screen script was rolling from the right of the screen to the left in large letters.

Murder at the National Shrimp Festival. Three known dead, many more injured. No known cause listed as yet for the tragedy. Stayed tuned to Channel 10 for latest news and updates.

"Scott, are you still there?" Jonathan asked as he tried to take everything in that he was seeing.

"I'm here. Do you see the news channel? Do you see what they're flashing across the bottom of the television monitor?"

"I see the news alert, but I'm not sure I understand it. Tell me what you know so far."

"Our office is the organizing body for the shrimp festival every year in Gulf Shores, and it is the most important event for raising revenue for Gulf Shores and the other municipalities in this area. We have over 250,000 people expected to show up every day for the festival and a headline like this could destroy our opportunity for profit this year, and possibly for years to come. Someone has to get to the bottom of this matter soon, or we could lose our shirts!" As Scott was ranting into the phone, Jonathan saw another call coming into his phone from the governor's office. He told Scott to hold for a moment, and he would get back to him shortly. Switching the calls on his cell phone, Jonathan answered the call from the governor's office.

"This is Jonathan Pembroke. Were you trying to reach me?"

"Please hold for the governor," was all the voice said. So, Jonathan held until he recognized Big Jim Flower's voice booming on the other end of the line.

"Jonathan, this is Governor Flowers, and I won't bore you with small talk this morning. Have you seen the newscast running on your local television station this morning?"

"About the deaths at the shrimp festival?"

"Those are the ones," he said. "My office has contacted the television station, and they are removing the notice that is now being broadcast all over the Baldwin and Mobile County areas, but they have already probably done unrecoverable damage to the festival this year. They will run a disclaimer in its place, but I don't know how successful that will be in restoring the faith in the festival this year. The good news, if there is any, is that national syndication has not picked up the story, and we are threatening them that if they run an unverified story about the shrimp festival that they will be liable in the millions of dollars if they are wrong, and the festival is damaged financially. That will hold them off for a while, but not forever."

"What do you want us to do, Governor?"

"I am officially hiring you to get to the bottom of this screw up and clarify things before the National Shrimp Festival is toast this year. Will you do that for us? We will pay your normal fee for your services if you'll take on this disaster for us."

"We will be more than happy to help, Governor. As far as fees are concerned, we are a self-funding non-profit corporation, and we don't take any fees or money for our services. What we will need from you is to be sworn in as special deputies of the governor's office, with ID cards and shields, and the authorization to speak and act on your behalf. We couldn't start any serious investigation until that is done, otherwise we could be held liable for stepping on toes down here, if you know what I mean." The governor was quiet for a moment and then boomed out his decision.

"It's 7:30 AM, and by 10:00 AM you'll have those credentials in hand. Just give me the names of those who need the IDs and badges. I'll have them made shortly and flown down to the Jack Edwards National Airport. Can you have someone there to meet my plane?"

"Absolutely, Governor. Just have someone call or text me at this number an hour in advance of it landing and I will have one of my detectives meet your man and get the credentials."

"You are officially hired to represent me, the governor's office, and the state of Alabama concerning the investigation at the National Shrimp Festival. If you need support from the AHP that can be arranged as well. They answer to me, and they outrank any other official government policing authority in the state of Alabama."

"That's good to know, Governor. We have set up an excellent working relationship with CPT Larry Phillips, the police chief of Gulf Shores, as well as many of the other small municipalities down here, but if we need the weight of your office behind some action we need to take, I won't hesitate to contact your office."

"Excellent. Now, my plane will touch down in Gulf Shores in less than two hours. My office looks forward to working with you, and you can call my personal cell number day or night if you need me to get personally involved." Jonathan thanked the governor, remembered that he had Scott on hold, and switched back to his call.

"Scott, I'm sorry I had to put you on hold, but that call was from the governor's office. He had hired our agency to get to the bottom of this crisis, and we will begin that process as soon as I can assembly my team this morning. I'll keep you informed as to how things are progressing."

"What about the local television station? Will they stop broadcasting their unfounded claims?"

"You might check out the television station again," Jonathan said. He had been watching when the scrolling message changed from the topic of murder at the shrimp festival to an explanation that the earlier message had been a mistake made by a local programmer. That ribbon would run for about ten minutes and then there would be nothing at all about the people who were being rushed to the South Baldwin Medical Center for treatment.

"How did you pull that off?" Scott asked in amazement.

"After all, Scott, when the governor's office calls and requests that you suspend such a statement until the facts can be verified, only a stooge would refuse to grant the governor's request."

"Will you take the case? We can't pay your agency much for your work, but we believe that we need someone looking out on our behalf in this matter."

"Scott, we are now officially working for the governor's office, so you don't have to worry about paying us for anything. Give me your contact information and I will have one of my detectives update you when there are newsworthy items to share. Otherwise, act like nothing has happened."

"That's going to be hard to do, considering that the local television station has already spread the rumor all over the Gulf Coast area." Scott was obviously upset, and Jonathan tried to calm him with his next statement.

"Scott, this is a resort town. It is 7:30 AM in the morning on a Sunday, and I doubt many people saw the first bulletin rolling across the bottom of their televisions. For the few who did, the disclaimer that is now being run should put most of them at ease. However, that disclaimer will only run for a few more minutes, and then there will be nothing at all about the story on the local news channels. That's the best we can do for now until we check things out and discover what is really going on. Please tell me what you know about people being admitted to the South Baldwin Medical Center." Scott told him that several people had been admitted to the emergency room and that two of them had died of some mysterious illness. Initially the physicians on call thought that they were dealing with food poisoning, a common occurrence at any food festival the size of the one happening in Gulf Shores, but the vitals of the two dead people were showing signs of arsenic poisoning. Hence, they overreacted and assumed everyone coming into the emergency room might have been poisoned."

"Scott, we will get to the bottom of the problem as soon as my team arrives, and we can get our investigation underway. Do your best to avoid talking to the press and try to stay calm until we can get a better handle on what is really happening at the festival."

"I'm just afraid the news might be true. It would destroy this festival for this year, and possibly for years to come," he moaned.

"Look, Scott. I had my entire agency down on the beach yesterday, and we ate all kinds of shrimp with all the trimmings. None of us got sick. There has to be a reason that just a few people are sick, and that some of them died. We'll check it out as soon as possible. That's all I can promise you at this time." Scott agreed that no one could do anything about those already suffering and dying in the emergency room, and he told Jonathan that he would do his best to quell any rumors until Jonathan's agency could decide what really happened at the festival. He hung up, and Jonathan decided it was time to wake his people, beginning with Maggie.

Jonathan went back into the bedroom prepared to wake Maggie, but he saw that she was sitting up and watching the television on the distant wall from their bed. Maggie gave Jonathan one of those looks when he walked back into the bedroom.

"Jonathan, what the hell is going on down on the beach?" Maggie asked. He suggested that she get up, get dressed while he made coffee, and that they call Jo-Ellen and Maria and ask if they minded coming in on Sunday to help with a crisis.

"It will make more sense to you if I explain everything in detail and not just hit the high points," he said. She agreed, slipped out of bed and into the bathroom, while Jonathan pulled on some clothes and phoned Jo-Ellen. Within the hour everyone was assembled on the balcony overlooking the Gulf of Mexico. Jonathan explained what had happened to everyone, and if his people were indicative of most of the people in Gulf Shores on a sleepy Sunday morning, very few people had even seen the first bulletin about sick and dying people at South Baldwin Medical Center.

“Do you think we might have ingested poison yesterday when we were eating shrimp at the beach,” Maria asked innocently.

“No, Maria, or you would be dead,” Jo-Ellen answered her calmly. Maria was laid back most of the time, but if she ever began to worry about anything in particular, it was difficult to get her to overcome that fear. Jo-Ellen was trying to put things in perspective with Maria, but she never knew if Maria totally understood her explanations.

“Here’s what we know at this point, and it’s not very much. I received a telephone call from the governor who was very concerned about a story that ran on the local television station this morning saying that several people had been poisoned at the National Shrimp Festival, and I received another call simultaneously from Ferdinand Scott, the artistic director of the shrimp festival, asking for our help in deciding what was really happening on the beach and at the festival.”

“Wow! I can’t believe I slept through the biggest story in Gulf Shores since we moved here last year,” Jo-Ellen said. “Are we going to work for the shrimp festival to figure out what’s happening?”

“Yes and no,” Jonathan said.

“Please explain,” Maggie said. “I think we all are happy to protect our home area, see that no ill repute comes to its reputation, and bring justice to whomever may be causing all the grief. Just who will we be working for?"

"This answer may sound trite, but we will be working for ourselves, with the blessings of Big Jim Flowers. Since we work pro-bono on every case, the thing we need from the governor's office is the authorization and credentials which will open each and every door we need to pass through to get this job done."

"And Ferdinand Scott? How do we include him in our findings?"

"He goes by Scott," Jonathan said.

"I would, too," Jo-Ellen said and laughed. "Who would name their kid Ferdinand. I'll bet he got his ass beat every day in grammar and middle school."

"Let's refocus on the subject at hand," Jonathan said. He didn't want anything distracting his detectives when time was of the essence.

"Okay, here are the tasks we need to perform quickly. Someone needs to contact the hospital personally and see what the status is of those patients who were admitted to the emergency room from the shrimp festival. The governor is sending credentials for all of us to use to open doors and keep local and uncooperating police jurisdictions off of us while we investigate. Jo-

Ellen, I want you to drive to Jack Edwards National Airport in Gulf Shores, meet the governor's private plane, pick up the identification packets, and then go by the South Baldwin Medical Center and try to manipulate some information from the hospital about those supposedly poisoned at the festival."

"That's a tall order, Jonathan," Maggie said. "Do you think Jo-Ellen can pull that off on her own?" Maggie wasn't doubting Jo-Ellen's abilities, but she wanted to be supportive of her if the situation called for backup.

"Here's what you do, Jo-Ellen. After you get the credentials at the airport, go directly to the hospital administrator's office. Bypass local security, doctors and nurses in control of their little fiefdoms, and confront the man at the top of the food chain. Explain to him that *the governor* wants this done, or *the governor* wants that done, and not that we are asking for exceptions to their rules. Imply that we will be happy to report his cooperation, or lack thereof, to Big Jim Flower's office when our investigation has been completed."

"And you think that will work?" Maria asked, now getting very interested in manipulating the hospital administration for their investigation.

"We have a 50/50 chance of it working, but since the public hospitals in the state rely on the government to supply funds to help deal with the uninsured and indigent patients, I would say we'll probably get some cooperation. I can't guarantee you how much." Jonathan's phone rang and it was Rocky Jones from the governor's office.

"Jonathan, this is Rocky Jones. I can't remember if we've worked together or not in the past, but I'm your designated 'go to guy' for this particular incident. I have the full authority of the governor, and your credentials should be arriving at Jack Edwards National Airport in the next thirty minutes. Please keep my office informed as things develop down there. The governor is very interested in the outcome of the investigation. You can contact me day or night," Rocky said, and he gave Jonathan his phone number and email address.

"Thanks, Rocky. Hopefully, we can keep this all on the QT until we figure out what's going on and why someone would want to damage the National Shrimp Festival's reputation."

"Is that what you think is going on down there?"

"It's always hard to say this early in an investigation, but there are only a handful of motives for people to do stupid things like what has been done this morning."

“Humor me and tell me what those motives might be.”

“Most crimes which involved serious injury, death, or capital theft losses fall into one or more of the following motives: greed, jealousy, envy, or revenge. These can overlap some, but usually someone serious enough to possibly kill innocents with poisons or other things that can be ingested, have big-time motives. It may take us a day or two to run down leads and see which way the investigation points, but I will keep your office in the loop.” Jonathan hung up, told Jo-Ellen to get moving towards the airport, and to check in as soon as she made contact with the hospital if she needed reinforcements to get the hospital administrator to cooperate with their investigation. She nodded her agreement, and then she disappeared into the elevator heading for her car.

Chapter 3

Official Business

While Jo-Ellen Broussard didn't have the maturity and extensive experience of her mentor, Maggie Watson, she could be formidable when she needed to be. She dressed well, was always neat in her appearance, and she presented herself with professionalism. While it was true that Jo-Ellen was gay and living with her significant other on a full-time basis, she didn't come across as harsh or belligerent like so many of the "woke" people did today. No one could look at Jo-Ellen and tell she preferred her sexual partners to be female, because Jo-Ellen didn't give off those vibes. She was hit on by men all the time, and she usually just brushed off the advances as nothing she would be interested in. Once in a great while a man might be too aggressive to suit her taste, and Jo-Ellen would put him in his place so quickly that his head would spin. She grew up in a house where she had been abused by her father and not protected by her mother. Her later years as a foster child had her feverishly working to become an adult as soon as she was legally able to do so. She would not be intimidated by a doctor, nurse, or administrator in the South Baldwin County Hospital.

Arriving at the small terminal at Jack Edwards National Airport, Jo-Ellen went ahead directly to the fenced area where the passengers walked to the planes to board. She was idling in her Mustang when a Bombardier private jet landed and taxied up to the deplaning area. The jet was painted the state of Alabama colors, and had the governor's office seal on the tail, so it was pretty clear that it was the courier for the governor's office. A man in a three-piece suit came down the ladder, walked over to the fenced gate, and asked if Jo-Ellen was the courier for the M&J Detective Agency, passed a large bubble-wrapped envelope to her, and he reboarded the plane. Shortly after his boarding, the Bombardier taxied down the runway quietly and lifted off in the of the runway for its return trip to Montgomery. Jo-Ellen was impressed that the governor would fly credentials down to them in a matter of hours at what had to be a great expense. The private jet cost approximately $4,000 per hour to operate, so just the cost of the jet itself was not what made it expensive to own and operate such a jet for a normal business. Jo-Ellen turned her attention back to the envelope, opened it gently, and saw four sets of credentials identifying everyone in the office, to include Maria Garcia, as a special deputized law enforcement member of the governor's staff. There were badges, identification cards, and leather wallets designed specifically to display both the badge and ID card at the same time. She took her credentials packet out of the envelope, place the shield and ID card in the wallet, and placed it in her pocket for quick identification should she need it. Jonathan had given her a monumental task of convincing the hospital administrator that the M&J Detective Agency had privileges which could be disputed, assuming one wanted to irritate the AHP and the governor's office. No, Jonathan wasn't worried about Jo-Ellen or Maggie pulling off a caper like that. They just were convincing in their approach to the situation which made authority figures trust them. Now armed with her new credentials, Jo-Ellen headed to the South Baldwin Medical Center. When she arrived, she parked in the section reserved for police officers only, locked up her Mustang, and headed inside to the information desk. Getting past the many gatekeepers designed to filter out the riffraff of the common man from the elite medical staff might be a problem with someone less aggressive than Jo-Ellen.

"Flashing her new credentials at the volunteer on the information and visitation desk, Jo-Ellen asked where she could find the hospital administrator's office. Rather than getting a clear-cut answer, the older woman on the desk asked Jo-Ellen's purpose for needed to know that information. Jo-Ellen didn't answer the question, but she posed one to the gatekeeper. Writing down her name, Jo-Ellen asked the woman if she liked working at the hospital?

"What an odd question for you to ask," Harriett McCloud responded to Jo-Ellen. "I'm not sure that's any of your business." This time when Jo-Ellen pulled the shield and ID card, she pointed out that she was a special agent for the governor's office, and she didn't have time to play their silly games.

"You can either put me in touch with the hospital administrator at once, or I can call the governor's office and tell him that you, Harriett McCloud, is obstructing justice even after you were informed of my special status with the governor's office. Which do you prefer?' The older woman looked as if Jo-Ellen had stabbed her with a sharp instrument.

"You don't have to get nasty," Harriett said. "I'm only doing my job."

"I'm sure that's correct, under normal circumstances, but right now I don't have time to argue the point with you. This is a matter of life and death, and if you delay me enough for it to cause someone to lose their life, which will be on you." Harriett picked up the receiver and called for the administrative assistant to the hospital administrator come to the information desk at once. In what seemed like seconds rather than minutes, a tall, middle-aged man appeared and asked Harriett what she needed.

"I'm sorry, but I didn't get your name," Harriett said to Jo-Ellen. Jo-Ellen told her, showed the new credentials to Lex Brown, the assistant to the hospital administrator, and asked to see whoever was the final authority at the South Baldwin Medical Center.

"My name is Lex Brown, the administrative assistant to Dr. Theodore Bratton, who is our chief administrator. How can we be of help to the governor's office?" he asked. Jo-Ellen showed Lex her credentials and kept them out long enough for him to see the designation of Special Investigator of the governor's office, and then she replaced them in her pocket.

"I represent the M&J Detective Agency, and we are here on behalf of the governor's office."

"How can South Baldwin Medical Center help you, Detective?" Lex asked.

"The governor's office has asked us to conduct a thorough investigation of those people who have been admitted or treated and released who have been at the National Shrimp Festival. We will need to speak to the doctors and nurses who treated them, as well as your lab director. Can you arrange that for me, or do I need to speak to your hospital administrator?"

"He's going to tell you exactly what I'm about to say. Because of HIPPA regulations, we cannot release any information about those individuals you speak of without their written consent." Smug in his practiced answer, Lex Brown stood in the hallway with his arms crossed over his chest.

"I was afraid you might say that" Jo-Ellen said, and she dialed their office in Gulf Shores.

When Maria picked up Jo-Ellen began her act. "Is this the governor's office?" she asked Maria.

"Are you trying to outsmart someone at the hospital?" Maria asked with a chuckle. "Should I call you back in a few minutes?"

"Absolutely. If he is tied up right now, please have him return my call. It appears that the South Baldwin Medical Center may have to be locked down either under martial law or a directive of Homeland Security. I will be at this number waiting for his call." Jo-Ellen hung up her phone, moved to a chair in the waiting room, and acted like she was waiting for the governor's office to return her call. All of a sudden, Lex Brown wasn't so confident or arrogant.

"Who did you just call?"

"Are you deaf as well as dumb?" Jo-Ellen was deep into her act now, and she was enjoying every minute of it.

"Wait, we can work something out, I'm sure of it," Lex now appeared to be begging. Just then, Jo-Ellen's phone rang. She answered it, said uh-huh three times, and then looked up at the assistant administrator.

"Let me ask him, Governor," Jo-Ellen faked a question to the imaginary governor on the phone. "What will it be, Mr. Brown? Do we send in the National Guard, or are you willing to cooperate? Do you want to talk to Governor Big Jim Flowers yourself?" Lex backed away as if the phone were a poisonous snake.

"No, no. Tell him that we will open our files to you at once. I didn't know we were talking about Homeland Security issues." Jo-Ellen thought to herself that this was almost too easy.

"Hold up, Governor. He says he will help us and cooperate. His name?" Jo-Ellen looked at Lex's nametag on his badge and read it out loud, as if someone on the other end of the line were writing it down at the same time. "I'll tell him, Governor." Jo-Ellen hung up her phone and thanked Lex for his expected cooperation.

"Where do you want to start first?" he asked timidly. Now that the lion had been tamed, Jo-Ellen could get on with her work. She didn't know how legal or illegal falsely saying that the governor of Alabama was backing them up, but she would go for "it's easier to get forgiveness than to get permission" in this case. Jo-Ellen requested to speak to the lab first, and then to the patients who had been admitted to the hospital and were still conscious and able to speak. Lex walked her down to the lab, told Jo-Ellen to have him paged when she wanted to see the patients, and he disappeared. Jo-Ellen didn't think that her cover had been blown, but she decided to work fast just to ensure she got all the available information before she was booted out of the hospital. Lex might have gone to his legal counsel and asked advice which could hinder Jo-Ellen's research. Jo-Ellen spoke to the lab technician.

"Can you tell me what made these people sick?" The lab tech was a typical scientist with no outgoing communication skills, but he did tell her what she needed to know.

"It looks like the two people who died did so of arsenic poisoning. The other ones who were sick had a variety of issues, from food poisoning to acute anxiety attacks."

"Just two individuals showed signs of arsenic poisoning. Are you sure?" The tech looked at Jo-Ellen and rolled his eyes.

"I'm sure. Now go away and let me do my job. I have several very sick people to diagnose the cause of their illnesses." He turned away from Jo-Ellen and began to busy himself with his petri dishes, flasks, and beakers. Realizing that she had been excused from the lab tech, Jo-Ellen made her way back to the information desk. She asked for the room numbers of those brought into the hospital who were believed to be suffering from food poisoning. She was immediately allowed to visit several rooms, speaking with those patients who were awake and aware, and speaking to the caregivers of those who were sleeping. After a thorough investigation of the waiting room, the ER department, and the lab, Jo-Ellen was on her way out the door of the hospital. The entire episode only took forty-five minutes. Jo-Ellen arrived back at the M&J Detective Agency office with the biggest win of her early private detective career.

"Okay, Jo-Ellen. What happened at the hospital?" Jonathan asked as he looked approvingly over the credentials the governor's office had sent them.

"I may have fudged the information a little bit, but when I met resistance from the assistant administrator, as he was spouting all the HIPPA information and why he couldn't cooperate with us, I told him that the governor's office had hired us to figure out the cause of the sickness generated at the National Shrimp Festival. When he further resisted, I called the office and role-played speaking to the governor's office with Maria. She picked up on it quickly and didn't blow my cover. Anyway, long story short, he gave me complete access to the lab as well as the affected patients who are still suffering from food poisoning."

"That's good, then. Just food poisoning and nothing sinister?"

"We should be so lucky. The lab tech, who by the way had the personality of a dead tree, told me that the two victims who had died had traces of arsenic in their systems. The others in the hospital now are either suffering from real food poisoning or they are hyperventilating about maybe having been poisoned. The hospital has not announced the cause of death of the two victims killed by ingesting poison at this time."

"We need to keep it that way for the time being. This looks like one of two things to me. Either someone is trying to damage the reputation of the National Shrimp Festival, or they are using this opportunity to possibly extort money from the festival by threatening a widespread outbreak of sickness and death."

"Which of those two things do you think it is?"

"I'm not sure at this point, but we definitely need to keep this on the QT until we know for sure what's happening. I will call Rocky Jones and have his office contact the hospital and ask them to hold off on notifying the local authorities and the news outlets that there have been two deaths due to arsenic poisoning."

"What if the hospital will not agree to cooperate with Rocky's office?"

"The state of Alabama supports the Baldwin County Medical Center with lots of funding, and that gives Rocky some short-term leverage. Of course, if this is an epidemic of poisoning, the public should be made aware of the possibility of harm coming from attending the shrimp festival. We'll just have to play it by ear but knowing that arsenic is involved speeds up our timetable to get to the bottom of this tragedy." Jonathan picked up the phone and dialed Rocky's personal cell number. After a brief conversation, Jonathan told Maggie, Jo-Ellen, and Maria that the governor's office could probably buy them two to three days' time before the public had to be notified.

"That's how long we have to solve these murders?" Maggie asked.

"It looks that way. The problem isn't just this week, or even this year, but the impact on the shrimp industry along the Gulf Coast could be irreparably harmed if this gets out before we can figure out what and who we are dealing with." Everyone nodded solemnly and began to work on a solution to the problem.

"What can I do, Jonathan, to help expedite good results?" Maria asked. She felt helpless stuck at a desk while Jo-Ellen, Jonathan, and Maggie were out combing the beaches for possible causes for the sicknesses.

"I think we need to know who the principal vendors are on the beach and near the beach. The city of Gulf Shores, Ferdinand Scott to be specific, should be able to get that information pretty quickly. To ensure that the city gets its fair share of tax revenue, all vendors must buy and openly display a temporary city license to sell anything on the beach or within the city limits of Gulf Shores and Orange Beach. See if you can get Scott to send you an authorized list of vendors for this year's shrimp festival. He should be able to pull that up in his computer and send you a copy in no time." Jonathan gave Maria the phone number that Scott had used earlier in the day to contact Jonathan and first report the problems on the beach.

"Jo-Ellen, please call CPT Lawrence Phillips of the Gulf Shores Police Department and ask him if we can hire his daughter Laurie to help us comb the beaches verifying who does and who doesn't have the proper authorization to do business during the shrimp festival. She can come over after school, assuming she's in school today. Many of the local school systems have allowed their students to take the day off and enjoy the local festival. Tell him we will pay her the normal hourly wage if he will allow her to help us."

"Maggie, you, Jo-Ellen, and I will comb the beach with an eye on deciding who has property applied and received a permit to do business during the festival, and who has not. That doesn't mean that someone who up to no go is not guilty of creating this terrible crime even though they are registered, but I would think if they planned ahead with the sole purpose of damaging the shrimp festival's reputation, the perp might take short cuts to try to keep from being tracked by the local authorities. Just showing up, setting up a similar booth to the other ones, and working like everyone else would give them immediate cover for their crimes."

"How many vendors do you think we need to check out? Will Scott have that kind of information?" Jo-Ellen asked. Maria spoke up before anyone could speculate more on that question.

"Scott said there were 2563 authorized vendors. Some with permits for tents, and some just with permits to sell their wares on the beach from a cart or whatever other vehicle that they may have available."

"In other words, everyone is a prime suspect who is on the beach?" Maggie sighed. "That's going to take us a while to figure out."

"With the four of us combing the beach, we can cover the festival grounds in three or four hours. We only need to see the permit or license posted in the vendor's area. If it is someone selling hats, scarf, or clothing items they would probably not have the means of poisoning anyone," Jonathan said. "We need to concentrate on food and drinks, popcorn and wine coolers, beer and ice cream vendors."

"Is that all?" Maggie quipped. She wasn't happy to be doing yeoman's work on this investigation. She would prefer that they hire more kids like Laurie to do the legwork. When she suggested it to Jonathan, he just shook his head.

"You are the professional, and we need your expertise more than just a few more people minimizing the effort to find the culprit." While Maggie didn't like the idea of using SPF-50 sunblock and walking for hours in the sand, she agreed that Jonathan was right.

Chapter 4
Exhaustion

Maggie had good reason to want some kids to do the dirty work of walking the beaches for hours, trying to separate the sheep from the goats. One of the first things Maggie had learned about her new adopted home was that the temperature was mild in the winter, warm in the spring and fall, and blazing hot in the summer, but it was humid 24/7, 365 days a year. An hour in the heat and humidity of the summer days could roast your skin, and you could become dehydrated in a matter of minutes in the direct sun, rather than in hours. Maggie enjoyed the sunshine, heat, and warmth of the beach—in small doses, but not to the extreme. What Jonathan was proposing for all of them was excruciating, and for the fair-skinned Jo-Ellen, it was dangerous for her to be exposed too long in the intense direct sunlight. They would use the highest SPF level of sunblock that they could find, cover up as much of their sensitive skin as possible, and take water and lotion reapplication breaks regularly. There was no guarantee that this routine would help them discover who might be the perp who poisoned the two victims who had died earlier in the day at South Baldwin Medical Center, but it was a start. Logic said that the person creating the havoc was probably not a registered vendor, but logic was not always king in situations like this. The headquarters of the

National Shrimp Festival had established itself in the parking lot of the Hangout, so the detectives decided to walk from the Crown Victoria Condominiums where they lived to the beach. The condominiums were literally built next door to the Hangout and the Pink Pony Pub, and the Gulf Shores public beach was the preferred walking place for Jonathan and Maggie when they took their aging West Highland Terrier for her daily stroll. Molly, now an elderly Westie, could only sustain a walk of half of what she could do as a young dog when they lived in Rowlette, and many times Jonathan would pick her up, cradle her in his arms, and carry her back to their condominium if Molly tired during their exercise session. Still, Maggie believed that Molly's life was much better when she got regular exercise, so they would walk from the Crown Victoria Condominiums, past the Pink Pony Pub nearby, in front of the Hangout, which was separated from the white sandy beach by a small parking lot and access road, west toward Ft. Morgan, and then return walking east on Highway 182 which connected all the barrier islands along the coast of Alabama and Florida. They had been walking that same route since the first day they moved into their new home eighteen stories above the Gulf Shores public beach.

Donned with large straw hats, SPF of 50, and fanny pouches carrying water, Jonathan and his detectives boarded the elevator and rode to the first floor of the building. They exited the building, walked west to leave the private property of their condo, and were immediately engulfed in thousands of people overflowing the public parking lots and eating establishments along the frontage of the beach.

"Wow," Jo-Ellen said. "I've never seen so many people in such a small area in my life!"

"It's worse on the beach," Maggie said. "This is the third National Shrimp Festival we've attended since we moved down here, and the crowds seem to get larger every year."

"From the size of this crowd, I am assuming that few people heard the story about food poisoning and the two deaths from yesterday's visitors to the festival," Jonathan said. "That's what Rocky Jones told me he would do, but I'm surprised hi pulled it off. It's difficult to impose one's will upon the press when it comes to free speech."

"He's not controlling them through the press, Jonathan. He's probably controlling them by threatening to take away the governor's office financial support if they don't honor their word that they gave to him."

"How much time did he say we would have to get to the bottom of things?" Maggie asked.

"He thought forty-eight hours, but we may get a break and have a little longer before the hospital notifies the press about the arsenic murders."

"I guess that shows us that money talks!" Jo-Ellen said with a smirk.

"Just be glad that we're on the right side of that action this time. Normally, we're the ones being hampered by the press getting in the way of our investigations. If the governor's actions will stave off the press for a few days, I'm all for it," Maggie said. She got a couple of amens from her fellow detectives as they walked toward the main booth run by the National Shrimp Festival office.

"Let me do the talking," Jonathan suggested as they approached a pretty young attendant in the tent, dressed in a festive pink and white dress. While the tent was just that, it was separated into two sections, with a back room divided by a heavy cloth floor to ceiling curtain. There was also air conditioning being piped into the tent from a portable generator found just outside of the tent. When they stepped inside the tent it almost felt cold to Jo-Ellen and Maggie.

"This is nice!" Jonathan said to Mary, the welcoming attendant in the tent. Mary smiled, gave them the spiel which she had memorize to say to everyone who frequented their tent, and asked them if they needed directions.

"How may I help you? I have a map of all of the booths which are offering food and other things along the beach. There is no admission to enter the festival, but be mindful where you park your vehicle, because the city of Gulf Shores uses this festival to raise revenue for their normal operations by ticketing illegally parked cars and truck." Mary droned on about this and that, and finally stopped talking. Jonathan nor his companions interrupted her until she had finished speaking.

"Is Lex Brown here today?" Jonathan asked. Mary looked suspiciously at Jonathan and asked him what his business was with the festival director. This didn't upset Jonathan because he knew besides being the cheerleader for the National Shrimp Festival, Mary was probably the gatekeeper to prevent those without official business from worrying her boss.

"Mary, I spoke with Lex earlier this morning. He called me and asked for my help. Please tell him that I am here with my detectives, and we will want to have a word with him before we start our investigation. If Lex is not here, please call him and let me speak with him. Time is of the essence." Throughout his statement to Mary, Jonathan never raised his voice or sounded impatient. However, Mary had to know about the dilemma that the festival was facing, and as gatekeeper for her boss, she could surely find him quickly.

"Will you please wait while I consult with him?" she asked sweetly.

"Absolutely." Mary was gone less than five minutes and a middle-aged man, clean-cut and somewhat handsome, appeared in the front of the tent. He proffered his hand to Jonathan, Jo-Ellen, and Maggie, and they all shook it. Jo-Ellen's gay radar went off when she noticed Lex's abnormal attention which he was showing to Jonathan. He also held his hand a bit longer than necessary, and patted Jonathan on the back a couple of times during their conversation about the festival and its problems. She didn't care, but being gay herself, Jo-Ellen was more sensitive about noticing such things. She was sure Jonathan had no idea of what she was thinking.

"Jonathan, it's so good to meet you and your agency's detectives," Lex said. "We really have a dilemma here to deal with. I just hope it doesn't damage this year and the future years' festival success."

"That's why we are here, Lex. We have all been deputized by the governor's office, and along with our normal detective shields and ID cards, we have special agent designation cards and badges which have been issued by the governor's office as well." Jonathan showed Lex the credentials, which were impressive.

"Do we know what happened or why anyone would want to harm innocent people at a fun festival? That just sounds crazy to me," he said, again touching Jonathan's arm as he spoke.

"Not yet, but we have a plan to determine what's happening, and we wanted to make sure you knew about it before we put it into action." Jonathan explained how he, Jo-Ellen, Maggie, and the police chief's daughter were going to comb the beach verifying that all the vendors working in the National Shrimp Festival were legitimate and had registered with the festival's office and the city of Gulf Shores. Jonathan also explained that his agency thought anyone who might be trying to harm the festival would probably avoid registering officially so there would be no way to track them in the system.

"Do you think that someone intentionally is going out of their way to harm the reputation of the National Shrimp Festival?" This appeared to be a new thought for Lex, and he was upset that they might be targeted for harm.

"No one knows what I am about to tell you but a few people at the hospital, my people, and now you." Jonathan paused for a minute to give his next comments more of a dynamic impact.

"What? Is there a plot afoot?" Lex said, and almost giggled. Jonathan knew the information he was about to share with Lex would take any silliness or coyness away from the director.

"Two participants in the festival are dead, suspected of being poisoned with arsenic." That's all Jonathan said, and the effect on Lex was traumatic.

"Are you sure? That is horrible! What are we going to do to protect the rest of the attendees from getting poisoned? Do we need to shut down the festival?" While Lex was asking his questions, he was literally wringing his hands constantly. He seemed to lose focus, so Maggie jolted him back into the present.

"Lex, calm down. There are over a quarter of a million people attending the National Shrimp Festival this year, and only a few have shown to have been poisoned with arsenic. There are other visitors who have gone to the emergency room for treatment for food poisoning, but I'm sure that happens all the time at these types of gatherings. Right?"

"Sure. We have had hundred every year we have held the festival. Usually it is due to overeating, too much sunshine and heat, and some hypochondriacs. Some people get sick because some of their family or friends get sick, but all of those people recover. We have had a few people get very ill due to an allergic reaction to eating shellfish, but most people know in advance if they have such a problem. We have EpiPens available at the medical tents that are placed strategically up and down the beach just for those types of reactions. It's never been a real problem, and I don't think anyone has ever died in the past because of such a reaction to eating shellfish here."

"There have been two, and only two, persons who have died who have attended the festival, and all of the other patients admitted to South Baldwin Medical Center appear to be improving from their bouts of illness."

"Why would someone only murder two people at an open festival like this one? They could have killed hundreds or thousands. It doesn't make sense."

"That's because you are thinking as a private citizen and a businessman. We think like detectives and the crooks who cause this chaos."

"You don't think they intended to kill more than two people? Why go to all that trouble to just kill a couple of people when the opportunity is far greater if they want to make some kind of social statement?"

"If all they wanted to do was kill people, they probably would have killed more than two people initially. What they may be doing is trying to get someone's attention."

"I don't understand. Why would they want to do something like that?" Jonathan thought that Lex was a little dense if he didn't understand bribery and extortion.

"Lex, many times people use situations like the festival to extort money from the sponsors, organizers, or the city where the festival is being presented. In this case, they may have planned to use the exposure of two people dying of arsenic poisoning as a threat for you to give them money or something else of value to make them go away."

"Oh, I hadn't thought of that. What if we don't meet their demands?"

"Then they might poison more people to damage your reputation and cause your festival extreme financial harm. There's no guarantee that

that's what they're intending to do at this point, but it's possible."

"How do we deal with something like this?" It was obvious that Lex was getting frustrating that this was not going to be an open and shut case of demand and settlement.

"We have a couple of options, and I want the police chief of Gulf Shores involved in our discussions of how we can possibly neutralize this potentially dangerous situation."

"Okay. I understand that. Should we go there, or will he come here?"

"I will need to contact him and see which works best for him, but in the meantime, my detectives will begin combing the vendor's booths to ensure that each and every one of them has a valid city permit and a National Shrimp Festival certificate to operate during the festival."

"Do you have any idea how many different places you are going to have to inspect?"

"Unless you have added any last-minute vendors, we know that 2563 city permits were issued. Some are for vendors selling hats, tee-shirts, and other memorabilia, but most of them are for vendor offering food and drinks."

"That's amazing that you already know so much about the festival," Lex said. Most of the vendors have been here before and presented their goods to the festival in the past. Should we be concerned about them as well as new entries?"

"The odds are that repetitive vendors are not the ones most likely to want to cause disruption to your festival or the festival's reputation, because they would be damaging one of the sources for their own annual income potential. However, we are going to look at every vendor, check everyone for a license and permit, and leave no stones unturned. This is too serious a case to be guessing someone would or would not want to harm the National Shrimp Festival or the city of Gulf Shores."

"You know we bring in a lot of revenue to the city of Gulf Shores each year. They sell the vendor licenses, and I was told by a reliable source that they earned $500,000 in revenue just from the sale of those permits. That doesn't count the parking fees and violations they collect from when people park in unauthorized areas."

"I understand that the National Shrimp Festival also makes a lot of profit from the festival. My sources tell me that you guys will clear $5 million this year alone."

"That's probably true, and what did you say your fee would be to help us?"

"We are a non-profit organization, and we don't charge fees for our services. We are independently funded through a foundation, and our focus will be on preventing further violence and death, as well as possibly catching the perps who are causing all the chaos."

"Okay. What is our next move?"

"I'm going to get my associates here busy checking out the vendors on the beach. Then you and I will talk to the police chief. Since there have already been two possible murders, we need to loop law enforcement into our plans. By the way, you wouldn't have a master map of all the assigned vendors locations, would you?"

"Yes, we do. What we have discovered over the past years is that vendors tend to take advantage of their neighbors to claim a better spot on the beach if they are not held to the location assigned. We have 'marshals' who are assigned specific areas of the beach to patrol, and they help keep order, help with sanitation, and other duties that are more custodial than otherwise. I'll get the map for you." Lex came back with a binder showing each section, the vendors assigned spots, and other data to help control the normal confusion which can happen at large gatherings.

"Can you send us this information to our cell phones in either a text or an email?" Jonathan asked.

"Mary can get that done for you. Just give her your information and she will send you a link to our website where all that data is listed."

"That way, we can pull up the map by quadrants and see if each vendor is where they are supposed to be. All our detectives carry iPads, and they will be able to pull up the map when needed," Maggie said. Lex told Maggie that Mary would get them in the system at once, and they would be able to begin checking the validity of the vendors' booths as they walked beach. Now that everything was set for Jo-Ellen, Maggie, and Laurie Phillips' phones, Jonathan turned to Lex and proposed that they give the police chief a call and loop him into their operation.

"That sounds good. I'll be happy to go to the city hall if necessary. I've met CPT Phillips in the past, but just in passing. I usually deal with the mayor's office when we set up everything for the festival each year."

"I'll call him and see what works best for him. He's very interested in this festival running smoothly, because the city benefits front the sales of licensing, the parking fees, and the city sales tax that is collected on every dollar spent during the event." Jonathan had CPT Phillips' office on speed dial, so he simply pressed the correct button and the chief's secretary picked up.

"Chief Phillips' office. How may I help you?"

"This is Jonathan Pembroke, and I need to speak to him as soon as possible. It's a matter of urgency."

"Just a moment. I think he's in his office." She transferred his call and immediately Jonathan was connected to CPT Lawrence Phillips.

"This is Chief Phillips. How may I help you?"

"Captain, this is Jonathan Pembroke, calling you from the beach and the National Shrimp Festival. Have you got a minute?"

"I always have time for you and Maggie, Jonathan. What's up?"

"We have a couple of things we would like to discuss with you personally, and we can come to city hall if that's more convenient for you."

"No, I would like to get out of the office and come to the festival. I haven't gotten there yet, and I want to get my annual dose of shrimp before they strike the tents and leave town. Where should we meet?"

"Lex Brown, the festival's director, has an office set up in a tent just behind the Hangout. You can't miss it. We'll be on the lookout for you. And, get this, it's air conditioned!"

"That sounds great. My uniform and the heat of the beach don't mix well. I'll be there in a few minutes. I'm leaving my office now." Jonathan thanked him and sat down in a one of the wicker chairs which were provided it the director's hut.

"Would you like something to drink while you wait on the chief?" Mary asked.

"That would be nice. What have you got?"

"Beer, wine, and bottled water. Which do you prefer?"

"I prefer beer, but I'd better stick to water. I'm officially working so I need to stay professional."

"It is a festival," she said. "No one would think bad of you for having a beer or a glass of wine."

"I'll stick to water, but thanks anyway." Mary produced a bottle of water so cold that it was sweating, and Jonathan took a big gulp. He had not realized that just being down here would be dehydrating, and he was thankful he chose water over alcohol. Ten minutes after Jonathan's conversation with the captain, he appeared at the tent and Jonathan formally introduced him to Lex Brown. They made a little small talk, but the issue was so pressing that Jonathan moved things along quickly.

"Captain, we need to share something with you which you probably don't know at this time. Lex called me this morning and asked for my help. He was told by the South Baldwin Medical Center that some of his patrons visiting the festival had gotten food poisoning and had been admitted for treatment. Knowing the sensitive nature of the matter, I had one of my detectives go to the hospital and ask them to keep a lid on thing until we could figure out the seriousness of the matter. After speaking to the lab tech, Jo-Ellen discovered that two of those suffering sicknesses died of what they think was arsenic poisoning. We are suppressing that information to the general public for fort-eight hours, or until we are certain that the arsenic poisoning was done as a leverage of some kind for whoever set this action in motion. The other people at the hospital were simply sickened by either eating too much food, drinking too much alcohol, or getting too hot while they were on the beach, or a combination of all three things." When Jonathan finished informing the captain about the circumstances, he wasn't sure how Phillips would react. Jonathan had taken the liberty to leave the chief of police, as well as everyone else in the city of Gulf Shores, out of the picture for several hours. He made a judgment call, and now was the defining moment.

"Normally, I would not appreciate someone assuming how I might handle a crisis like this, but I do understand how important keeping a lid on something like this can limit the overall damages to the festival. I'm not sure how the governor's office would react to how we've handled it so far, but I think you've done a pretty good job keeping things under control. Of course, you could have told me all of this over the phone, so I'm imagining that you have a plan going forward which includes the city?"

"That is right, Chief. We think we are dealing with someone who either has a grudge against the National Shrimp Festival or the city of Gulf Shores."

"Why us? What could they possibly have against us?"

"I don't have specifics, but if the city is benefiting from the parking fees, local taxes, and parking violations, that's a lot of money for a small city to lose. While I don't think that you are the target of the hoax, you would be greatly affected by the loss of revenue."

"That's for sure. How can the city help without getting in your way?"

"We have 2563 vendors who supposedly have bought licenses and permits to sell their goods on the beach. I have Maggie, Jo-Ellen, and your daughter Laurie performing a sector-by-sector inspection of every vendor on the beach. If you could spare two or three plain clothed officers to help us search it would make things go much faster. The sooner we prove, or disprove, my theory that it's probably an unlicensed vendor creating all the havoc with the festival, the sooner we can adopt a plan to put him under arrest and secure the event. There's just too much financial loss or gain riding on this to not take it most seriously."

"I agree. I'll send you some people within an hour or two, or just as soon as I can figure out who I can spare. What do you plan to do when you are pretty certain who the perp is?"

"We're going to have to play that part by ear and adjust our response as we go along. I will keep you in the loop, and your people can communicate with your office with their radios. It goes without saying that this particular perp is dangerous and should be treated as hostile. He's surely already responsible for two deaths by arsenic poisoning." The chief agreed, everyone shook hands, and Jonathan prepared to contact his people and bring them up to date on the new wrinkle in their plans.

Chapter 5
A Coordinated Effort

Operations that take place over a long amount of time or a vast amount of territory take extra coordination to make them work properly. It's like the difference of putting together a jigsaw puzzle of ten pieces verses 10,000 pieces. They are both tasks that needed coordination, but the latter requires much more patience and effort than a simple puzzle of just a few pieces. The puzzle that the M&J Detective Agency were trying to solve was massive in its logistical challenges, but still a logical and methodical approach could get the job done successfully. The big unknown factor possibly working against Jonathan and his detectives was the element of time. Forty-eight hours was not much time to cover all the ground which they had to do and still complete the task successfully. If things went bad and more lives were lost because the press had not been notified about the poisoning at the National Shrimp Festival someone's butt would be in a sling, and it would probably be CPT Phillips. He was the ultimate authority for local law and order, and now that he knew the facts, he could no longer plead ignorance of the crimes. Larry Phillips had the ultimate respect and loyalty to Jonathan and the M&J Detective Agency, and he just hoped his willingness to go along with Jonathan for the time being wouldn't jump up and bite him on the butt!

He had sent three of his patrol officers to help in the search for a possible imposter with a sales booth on the beach. They didn't know what they were looking for, but they knew each vendor had to have a permit and a temporary license to do business during the shrimp festival. Although they were plain clothed officers, they did each have their service weapon strapped on their hip, advertising that they were not there just for fun and games. It was a gentler way to enforce the law without stirring up too much interest in the officers helping in the search.

"Maggie, Jo-Ellen, and Laurie," Jonathan called into his two-way radio which he had secured for each of them before they began their search of the beach. He waited for each of them to call back acknowledging his page. One by one they all responded with 10-4. That was the uniform response on every police radio which Jonathan and Maggie had ever worked.

"We have a situation. Chief Phillips is offering three of his people to help us search the vendor's booths for credentials. Please let me know specifically where you are in your sector, and I will assign each of them to begin working your same sector from the opposite end of the beach. Got it?" The response from each one was the same as last time, along with the coordinates of where each was physically in her search. Jonathan wrote it all down, transmitted the information to the city of Gulf Shores dispatcher, and she, in turn, notified the undercover officers where they were to position themselves for the search. So far, so good.

Going code 10-11, meant that the officer was in service, but was on a special assignment. Jo-Ellen, Maggie, and Laurie all responded back to Jonathan with 10-11 answers to his inquiry. They now had enough manpower to effectively verify the licenses and permits each vendor had to have bought to be registered and authorized to operate during the National Shrimp Festival. Jonathan had removed himself from the search committee since CPT Phillips had supplied the extra manpower. He wasn't sure what it would mean if and when he found unregistered vendors, but as those things developed, he would deal with them. So far, his guess had been pretty accurate. No more deaths from arsenic poisoning probably meant that someone would be getting a threat notification soon.

"Jonathan, you didn't say how we should handle the situation if we discovered someone without credentials working during the festival. Should we shut them down and impound their provisions?" He had to think a minute before he answered Maggie.

"That may be too aggressive a place to start enforcement. It would be better if we had a better picture of the violator before we put them in the stocks!" he chuckled as he made the comment. According to Wikipedia, the stocks consist of placing boards around the ankles and wrists, while with the pillory, the boards are fixed to a pole and placed around the arms and neck, forcing the punished to stand. Victims may be insulted, kicked, tickled, spat on, or subjected to other inhumane acts.

"Good idea," Maggie said. Jonathan's humor never evaded her, but sometimes she thought it was misplaced in serious situations. "What shall we do then?"

"Show your credentials, take a picture of the vendor's stand, and make sure you get a facial shot of the operator. Tell him to cease and desist from selling his goods until he has checked in with the National Shrimp Festival office, obtained a permit, and paid the city of Gulf Shores for a temporary license to use his booth. Only if he gets hostile do you physically restrain him in any way. In that event you can handcuff him, radio me the circumstances, and I will notify one of CPT Phillips' officers to pick him up and take him to city hall. How they deal with him from that point on will be their call and not our problem." Maggie agreed and signed off the two-way radio band. Jonathan contacted the other five detectives and police officers and gave them the same instructions. Everyone came back "10-4," so Jonathan figured he had put the word out as best he could. The last thing he wanted to do was cause a scene on the beach while they were quietly trying to find the perp who may have poisoned the two innocents who now lay on a cold metal gurney in the basement of the South Baldwin Medical Center's makeshift morgue.

"Jonathan," the familiar sounding voice sounded on the other end of the phone line. "It's Maria, and I think you should come back to the office for a few minutes and look at a message I just received on our open office phone line."

"It's not something you can tell me on the phone?"

"I'd rather not. It's of a very sensitive nature. These cell phone lines are not secure. I think you will be glad you came back to the office to see it." Jonathan agreed, and he walked back over to the office from the beach. As he headed back to their condominium building, it seemed to Jonathan that the massive crowd of people had grown even larger. He boarded the dedicated elevator to their suite, and in seconds he was exiting the elevator into the foyer of their condominium office suite.

"What's up?" he asked casually as he approached Maria's desk.

"Listen to this," she said, and she punched the replay button on the answering service connected to their telephone line.

"I am going to remain anonymous to you for the present time, but you should listen closely to what I am about to tell you. It's time for big government, and big business, to yield to the will of the individual, give back profits from unfair

price gouging, and stop oppressing people's God-given rights. Two people have been sacrificed to get your attention, but we can sacrifice more if that's what it takes to make you do what's right. We have demands, and we will make those shortly, but don't be deceived. This is not a hoax, nor are we going to be satisfied with a token gesture of repentance on your part. You were hired to find us and put things back into place that will make the National Shrimp Festival a safe and fun place again. Good news. You found us. Now watch for our next instructions."

"There was no name or other identifying information attached to the message. I called our phone tracing service, and the call was made from a burner phone, and the signal was triangulated to the public areas of Gulf Shores Beach, but that's the best they could do. According to the service, the phone is now somewhere in a stationary place, and it hasn't been moved since the call was made. The odds are that the perp threw the phone away in one of the trash receptacles on or near the public beach area. That's all I have."

"You were correct in not sharing that information over an unsecured phone line. What we will have to do is bring the police chief into the investigation now and get his thoughts on how to move forward."

"I thought you were leaving them out of this operation," Maria said.

"That's before it became extortion. Extortion, kidnapping, murder, and blackmail are offense which ramp up the seriousness of a crime. At this point, the police chief has to decide whether or not to get the F.B.I. involved, or just let things play out as they come. I think once we hear the demands of the perp that we will have a better idea of who needs to be informed of the crisis."

"What do we do now?"

"The most difficult task any private detective every has to do—wait!" Jonathan boarded the elevator, left the office, and transmitted a general message to all six of his people looking for festival rules violators.

"This is headquarters. Code 10-19 to the parking lot of the Hangout. ASAP. Please acknowledge." He received six "10-4" messages in return. Jonathan went into the Hangout and secured a large booth for his team. In a matter of minutes, they began trickling into the air-conditioned space. Everyone seemed happy to be enjoying being out of the heat and the sunshine. Once everyone was seated around the table, the waitress took their drink orders and scurried off to fill their requests. Jonathan introduced the city of Gulf Shores police officers to Jo-Ellen, Maggie, and Laurie. Laurie knew them because she had worked in her dad's office and saw them regularly in the precinct.

“It’s not that we’re complaining, but why have you called us together?” Maggie asked. Everyone else nodded similar sentiments.

“We have had an interesting development, and I thought you should be the first to know. As soon as I’m finished briefing you on the information, I will be speaking with CPT Phillips, and we hope to put together some strategic plan to help us figure out who the perp is. Our office just received a phone message declaring responsibility for the two murders on the beach yesterday. While the note was vague, we believe the person who left it is somehow involved with the incident yesterday, and we further believe that he or she will try to contact us again soon. This appears to be an effort at extortion, and that’s why the police department must be more involved at this point of the investigation. On another note, did any of you discover people running a booth or vendor tent without authorization? If so, raise your hand.” Every hand went up. Jonathan gave the M&J Agency phone number to the three Gulf Shores police officers, and he asked each of them to call Maria with their facts. “Maria will compile a list of those who are skirting the system to make added profits, and that information will be given to CPT Phillips to share with his interdepartmental people. Did anyone see anything exceptionally suspicious?” No one answered yes to that question.

"We have worked approximately half of the beach tents and vendors, so another couple of hours will probably be sufficient for us to wrap up this portion of the investigation," Maggie said. "Shall we say that we'll meet back here in this air-conditioned place around 3:00 PM to combine our results?" Jonathan agreed, and the six investigators left the comfort of the Hangout, and they were soon back into the high temperature, high humidity of the public beach area. It was time for Jonathan to call CPT Phillips. Jonathan listened to the phone ring in the chief's office, and then a familiar voice answered.

"Chief Phillips. How may I help you?"

"Chief, it is Jonathan Pembroke. We need to sit down again and speak to you, and I don't want to share the facts I have over the phone. Again, I can come to town if coming to the beach is an inconvenience to you."

"I'll come there. It's about lunchtime, so we can meet somewhere and eat and discuss your thoughts at the same time. Where shall we meet?"

"Well, you have Hooters, the Pink Pony Pub, and the Hangout to choose from to eat lunch. Which do you prefer?"

"If I remember, the Pink Pony Pub has the freshest seafood along the Gulf Shores Public Beach area. Let's meet there. It's such a nice fall day, maybe we can eat out on the deck overlooking the Gulf of Mexico."

"I'll make it happen. I'll walk over and get us a good table before the rush begins. I'll order us an appetizer to get us started as well." The chief hung up, grabbed his hat and utility belt, and headed for the door. He told his secretary where he was going and how he could be contacted in case of an emergency, and then he got into his patrol car and headed south toward the beaches. When CPT Phillips arrived at the restaurant, he saw Jonathan sitting outside under a large umbrella, sipping on a large glass of something cold. He assumed it was iced tea.

"Hey, Jonathan," the chief said to him as he walked over to this table. The tide was coming in and the wavs were making so much noise that they could scarcely hear themselves converse. He and Jonathan exchanged pleasantries and shook hands.

"I'm having a Roy Rogers! Would you like one?"

"I don't think I even know what a Roy Roger's drink is!" the chief said.

"Basically, it's cola, grenadier syrup, garnished with a maraschino cherry. Quite tasty, if I do say so myself."

"I'm diabetic. Do you think that they could make it with diet soda?"

"Absolutely." Jonathan called the waiter over and gave him their drink order. He asked for a second Roy Rogers for himself.

"What's good to eat here? Laurie and I have eaten here in the past, but it's been a while."

"If you don't mind me ordering for both of us, I'll get us more to eat than we should have!" Jonathan motioned the waiter back over to the table, ordered the family platter of fried seafood, fries, hushpuppies, and Cole slaw."

"I'll bet this food is even better with a beer," the chief said.

"With beer or wine, the seafood here is excellent. It will be okay with our Roy Rogers drinks. This food is great with water!"

"So, what do we need to discuss concerning the National Shrimp Festival?"

"Our combination crew of my detectives and your police personnel have uncovered several vendors on the beach who are scamming the system—not buying permits or licenses to use at the National Shrimp Festival. We didn't want to make a fuss without consulting with your office, because we really have no authority to stop them from taking part in commerce on a public beach. You do since you have the authority to regulate commerce in your city, so we wanted to ask how you prefer us to handle these incidents?"

"Do you have a specific number of violators?"

"We've only covered about 50% of the area at this time, and we have discovered fifteen such vendors. If the margin stays the same throughout the search, I image you're looking at a little more one percent of illegally operated businesses."

"Of course, we hate to miss the revenue on any of those operating outside of the guidelines, but more importantly it gives others the idea that they can avoid following the rules as well, and one day you have a totally uncontrollable festival. We need to make an example of those vendors, but not punish them too harshly.

"It sounds like you have something in mind already," Jonathan said.

"For them to be able to remain in the festival as vendors, they need to pay a $100 fine to the city of Gulf Shores, buy a license and permit for their booths, and then they can continue to work. We will hold no grudges or punish them beyond the small fine. If they refuse, they must vacate their location on the beach within two hours of their refusal to comply. My officers will enforce the action so your people won't have to get involved." Jonathan acknowledged the chief's order and Jonathan said that he would relate it to all six of those seeking violators.

"To prevent them having to go back to the vendors a second time, they can inform the vendors as they find them in violation of the ordinance, and that should save some time."

"But does that get us our perp?"

"Probably not. After hearing the phone message which I told you about, I believe we will hear of a ransom or extortion plot to remove the danger from the festival."

"And do we pay them?"

“No so fast, Captain. These negotiations can get tricky and must be handled with kid gloves. The perp wants something in return for promising to not endanger any more lives, but the price may be too much to pay.”

“Do you think they will want money?”

“It’s difficult to say until they make their demands. Let’s take it a step at a time. The perp has promised that they will take no other action against the festival and the city of Gulf Shores until we have either accepted or rejected their demands. That could be today or tomorrow. We must be patient.”

“Why today or tomorrow? Why not next week?”

“How long does the National Shrimp Festival last?” The mayor began to nod his head in acknowledgment of what Jonathan was trying to say.

“It runs for four days. This is day two. There are only two days left, after today, for him to use the festival as a leverage against us or the city of Gulf Shores.”

“Exactly. That’s why I think we will hear back from him later today, possibly in the evening. That timeline would give him time to extort you, a day for you to comply, and a day for the festival to continue undamaged from bad news. His timing has been stellar to carry out whatever he has set out to do. You’re damned if you comply, and damned if you don’t.”

"But should we comply?"

"Yes and no. If we can convince the blackmailer that we are going to comply, but that it is going to take longer to get him what he wants, that will buy us some time to find him in other ways."

"Isn't that taking a risk?" the chief asked.

"Absolutely. The way I see it, Chief, we all take risks every day we walk out of our homes, get into our automobiles, and take to the highways. Your risk is obviously higher than something I just mentioned, but otherwise you have no idea the perp will follow through in good faith to do what he has promised even *after* you've followed his demands. That's one of the reasons the federal government never negotiates with terrorists. They are not dependable trading partners in any scenario, much less if they have already received national attention for their bad deeds. Once they have their money or whatever they ask for, they can then execute their hostages in public without any retaliation concerns. We must think of the person who has upbraided the National Shrimp Festival as if he were a terrorist, because that's what he really is."

"What do you suggest is our next move, Jonathan?"

"Unfortunately, Captain, we don't have the next move. The person or persons who poisoned the two innocents at the National Shrimp Festival has the next move. We will need to respond carefully, but without fear, if we are going to prevent this festival from turning into a national disaster."

Their food was delivered to the table and they both ate voraciously. When the platter was empty, the chief looked at Jonathan and made an astute comment.

"I can't believe we ate the whole thing!" he said and chucked.

"Just see what can be done when one puts his or her mind to accomplish a task," Jonathan said in return. "Have faith, Larry, we'll get his guy." It was one of the few times that Jonathan had purposely removed the official barrier between the two men, but he wanted the chief to know that Jonathan was personally committed to getting the job done right.

"I know you will, Jonathan. Now, I must get back and make sure the inmates aren't destroying the jail!" They both laughed at the ridiculous thought that anything so sinister could happen in Gulf Shores. Jonathan settled the bill, over the objections of the police chief, and they walked out to the parking lot.

"I swear this crowd is getting larger and larger every time I get away from it and return. You can almost stir these people with a stick."

"Let's just hope we can find the perp before he ruins everything for those who have come a long way to enjoy the dying days of summer with a bunch of shrimps!" Jonathan agreed, shook his hand, and the chief got into his patrol car and slowly made his way back to Highway 59 North which would take him back to his office.

Chapter 6
Punishment

Dostoevsky wrote the novel *Crime and Punishment* as his second novel, following his return from ten years of exile in Siberia. It has been considered one of the masters of mental anguish and moral dilemma expression, and therefore is a philosophical and psychological murder fiction novel. Published originally in 1866, the main character, Raskolnikov, turns from his law profession to a life of crime, including theft and murder. Although the plot and story are too convoluted to go into depth here, the main theme in the novel is the main character's alienation from society. We don't know what actions trigger a feeling of alienation for people, and it is totally an unpredictable outcome that can be expected when there is a psychic break in a person's mental capability to know right from wrong. Jonathan wasn't sure if that's what they were dealing with regarding the deaths at the National Shrimp Festival, but who logically and in their right minds poison people with arsenic just to get the attention of someone in charge of a festival like the one currently going on in Gulf Shores?

It was time to call his troops together and decide how to deal with those who have been scamming the festival's licensing and permitting process. They should be finishing up their rounds and at least they'll have an idea of how many people will be on their initial suspect list. If Jonathan had been a betting man, he might have predicted that he would hear from the extortionist by sundown that day, and he would have won that bet big! Jonathan had returned to the National Shrimp Festival headquarters tent to inform Lex Brown what the police chief and Jonathan had come up with as a rudimentary plan to detect and arrest the perp who was causing all the grief. He had been back from lunch with the chief only an hour or so when his cell phone rang again. This time Jonathan recognized the number on the screen of his phone as the M&J Detective Agency, so he spoke directly to Maria when he picked up the call.

"Maria, what's up?" he said, surprising her a bit.

"You were correct, Jonathan. We have received another message from the perp, but this time it was sent from a blind email account."

"Blind email account? What do you mean?"

"I don't know how they did it, but it appears the email came from us and was sent to us. Damndest thing I've ever seen."

"Forward it to me on my company email account, and I will look at it and see if I can figure out what he is asking for."

"Done," she said. "Check your email account and you should see it." Jonathan saw it and told Maria that he had received it. She told Jonathan that she would be at the desk until her normal 5:00 PM, as usual, unless you need for me to stay longer."

"That's fine, Maria. I imagine Jo-Ellen will get home by 6:00 PM. We're wrapping things up for the day really soon. I'll send her directly home to you."

"Thanks, Jonathan," was all Maria said in response. She was still quiet and shy, and Jonathan didn't expect any more from her than how she responded. Jonathan opened the email that Maria had sent to him, and he was just beginning to read it when he got a call from Maggie.

"All of us are at the end of the beach where the festival has been mapped out by the city and the organizers of the National Shrimp Festival, so I guess we've check everyone out. Should we meet back at the Hangout and tie up the loose ends?"

"That would be good. I'll got get us a table big enough for all of you. I guess we should buy dinner for everyone who helped us cover the territory. Why don't you get on your two-way radio and tell everyone to meet us at the Hangout as soon as they are able?"

"I will do that. Anything happening on your end?"

"In fact, there is, but I don't want to talk about it over an unsecured phone connection, nor do I want the city police officers to be privy to that information until I've gone over it with CPT Phillips."

"When did you get the new information?"

"Maria just received an email from the perp, and she sent it to me. Once we have dispersed our city helpers, the four of us will talk about things. Just get them into the Hangout so we can move on." Maggie told him she understood the expediency and would get it done as soon as she hung up from speaking with Jonathan. He left the festival headquarters booth and walked across the parking lot to the Hangout, secured a big table in the back of the restaurant. As the detective and patrol officers trickled in, Jonathan ordered each of them their preference of drink while the seafood platters were being prepared for their table. He encouraged them to have a glass of wine or a beer since they were now officially off-duty for the day. Jonathan didn't have to mention that suggestion but once, and soon the waiter was bringing a tray full of beers and wine glasses to the table.

"I have ordered three seafood platters for us to have for dinner. Take it from me, that will be enough food for all of us. I also ordered fries and hush puppies all around. By the way, have you people ever heard how hush puppies got their name?" Jo-Ellen and Maggie rolled their eyes since they had heard that corny story so many times that they could tell it from memory. But they laughed along with Laurie and the city police officers when Jonathan reached the punchline. Jonathan suggested that everyone call Maria before 5:00 PM that day so she could compile a list for

CPT Phillips to use to ensure everyone checked into the city's revenue office to buy their licenses and permits to continue to operate at the National Shrimp Festival. Everyone agreed to get the task done after they had dinner, and that's when the food came, and came, and came! Everyone's eyes were popping out of their heads at the volume of food placed in front of them. Shrimp of every kind, grouper, red snapper, oysters, crab claws, hush puppies, and fries were heaped on the trays in front of them, and they all dug in with gusto. There were stories of vendors trying to hide from the inspectors, running away from their stands, and one vendor breast-feeding her baby while they instructed her that she had to have a permit to run her stand. She promised to get it done as soon as the "feeding" was completed. As they finished up their dinner, Jonathan reminded each of them to contact Maria and give her their information. He pulled Maggie aside and told her that they had heard from the extortioner once more, but that the four of them would discuss it as soon as they were alone. She acknowledged his message, and she whispered it to Jo-Ellen and Laurie so they would be prepared to stay a few minutes when Jonathan dismissed the other officers. After everyone had shamelessly eaten everything on the three oversized platters which were brought to the table, Jonathan thanked them, and sent them back to the station or to their homes, depending on who was still on the clock. Jonathan asked each of them to call Maria quickly and give her their data, and soon everyone was back at the table, sipping on drinks and feeling overstuffed with seafood of every kind.

"I can't believe I ate all that fried food," Jo-Ellen said. "I'm going to get fat hanging around you, Jonathan." He smiled, tipped his beer mug towards her, and then took a big gulp. Jo-Ellen couldn't figure out how Jonathan could eat all that rich food, drink all the alcohol which he did on a regular basis, and still remain so thin. "You must have a hollow leg, Jonathan. If I ate like you do every day, I would be a size 22!"

"Is that big?" he asked innocently.

"Imagine Maggie being twice her size, and you'd be close."

"Just more to love," he smiled and gave his best girl a kiss on her cheek with his greasy lips. She didn't resist him, because he knew she loved him as much as he loved her.

"So, get to the big news about the email which Maria received. Will it help us figure out who the perp is?" Maggie asked.

"I'm forwarding it to each of you, so you can help me decipher it." The note was odd, but Jonathan was sure that they would be able to figure it out. It read:

"Don't look for me in the crowds, and don't look for me in the bars, but look for me in the eyes of those who have been abused over the years by those in authority. Payback is a bitch. Minimize

your losses by making restitution to those who have been abused, beginning with the people who work the National Shrimp Festival behind the scenes, those people who are taxed without representation, like those good citizens of Boston when all the tea was dumped into the harbor. Begin your reparations by setting up a fund at a local bank for those less fortunate than you. If you have not shown consideration for these requests within the next twenty-four hours, unfortunately more collateral damage may occur."

Like the last message, there was no one claiming to have sent it, nor who was behind the extortion. Even the requirement for setting up an account at a local bank was vague. Jonathan calculated that they had less than twenty-four hours to show good faith to the perp, or more innocent people might die as punishment for their lack of carrying out instructions. Each of the detectives read the email, but no one could say with certainty what the message meant.

"What happens in twenty-four hours if we haven't established an account at a bank for this perp?" Laurie asked.

"We'll set up an account, but no one outside of Maggie and I will have access to the funds I deposit into it. At that point we are at a loss of which way to continue at this point," Jonathan said.

"How do we notify him that we have complied with his demands?" Jo-Ellen asked. "Do we run a blind ad in the newspaper like we did in Ashburn and hope that he reads it?"

"For some strange reason I can't explain," Maggie said, "I think this perp has covered all his bases, and he will know if we have done as he requested."

"Is that hunch based on something other than your gut?" Jo-Ellen asked.

"In a way, Jo-Ellen. However, if this guy didn't tell us how to communicate our efforts to follow his requests, he will have access to knowing if we did as was asked. I fear that we are not dealing simply with someone with a grudge against someone at the festival or the city of Gulf Shores. It's bigger than that."

"You don't think you can fool this guy into thinking that we have cooperated when we really haven't?" Laurie asked. "Do really smart people do dumb things like poisoning people just to draw attention to themselves? I thought that kind of thing only happened on television."

"Unfortunately, that's not the case. There are some really messed up people walking the city streets of our nation with intent to harm other people just for the reason that they can," Jo-Ellen said. "Hopefully, we will intercept this guy before he hurts or kills anyone else during the National Shrimp Festival, but many times no matter what we do, people still get hurt. It's very frustrating."

"I guess I have a lot to learn," Laurie said.

"You do," Maggie said, "but don't ever become insensitive to others who purposely harm innocent people for no good reason. You should always get upset when something like the deaths of the two people from arsenic happen at a festive gathering. I've been at this detective thing for over twenty years, and I never get accustomed to murder and mayhem caused by others who feel justified to play God and decide whether someone lives or dies. It's just not natural."

"You're a senior this year, aren't you?" Jo-Ellen asked Laurie.

"I am. I'm looking forward to attending Ashburn University and studying Criminology there. I haven't decided whether I want to go on and get a law degree or not, but I will definitely graduate with a degree in Criminology."

"Why criminology?" Maggie asked. "Did your dad talk you into that major at school?"

"Heavens, no!" Laurie said. "If anything, he tried to talk me out of it. I think he's afraid I might get hurt or killed and he would be left all alone since mom died a few years ago."

"Take it from me, Laurie. You should pursue your goals, no matter who tried to dissuade you."

"You seem to be speaking from experience. What happened when you were growing up?"

"I grew up in a very strict home, went to Roman Catholic parochial schools until I graduated from high school, and I was never encouraged to attend college where I could study Criminology. The nuns kept steering me into home economics or other domesticated programs, and I kept telling them that I wanted to become a famous detective one day. They went as far as discouraging me from attending Loyola University in Chicago because I wanted to study Criminology, and they discouraged me from applying for a scholarship to that university. They were as surprised as I was when I got a full-ride scholarship from Loyola University, and they still told me that I would regret my decision as my life unfolded."

"Have you been disappointed in your life since graduation?" Jonathan joined in the conversation at that point.

"Maggie only had one dream her whole life, and that was to become like her namesake, Dr. John Watson, of the Sherlock Holmes novels created by Sir Arthur Conan Doyle in the early twentieth century. I tried to distract her when she was an undergraduate and she blew me off like a schoolboy," Jonathan smiled. "I had to pursue her after I completed a master's degree in psychology, and my law degree at Harvard. Still, she was hard to distract," he said. Maggie added to their story while sipping on a wine cooler.

"Jason chased me until I caught him," she laughed, and she planted a big kiss on his cheek. He blushed a little, but everyone could see that he adored the attention she was paying him. Laurie asked an innocent question which caught everyone off guard.

"Why aren't you two married?" Laurie asked. Maggie looked at Jonathan and he returned the look. Neither knew exactly what to say. Maggie finally answered the question as best she could.

"Johnathan and I have been engaged for several years, but we just haven't seen the need to make things official. I have a diamond engagement ring, which I never wear, which will blind you if the sun catches the stones just right. We'll get around to marriage one day, but neither of us is in a hurry."

"What do you think about that, Jonathan?" Laurie persisted.

"Whatever Maggie said goes fine with me." He took the easy way out, but he was actually being honest. He didn't worry about either of their loyalties to one another, and he was living with Maggie in a resort area, enjoying a special relationship with her, and he would never push Maggie to tie the knot until *she* suggested it.

"Enough about our love life," Maggie said. "Now let's figure out what message the perp intended for us to understand from his email."

Chapter 7
Reading the Tea Leaves

Trying to decipher the email the perp had sent to the office was like a gypsy trying to read tea leaves at the state fair. It looked good to the untrained eye, but could a gypsy really see the future or past in tea leaves or coffee grounds? It was too absurd to take seriously. The email was another matter. It was written almost as a riddle, but there was more to it than just a verse and rhyming meter.

"What does the perp mean when her or she says, *'Don't look for me in the crowds, and don't look for me in the bars?'* Does that mean he or she will not be out and about during the festival? Will they be plotting their evil scheme from somewhere other than the National Shrimp Festival in Gulf Shores?" Maggie asked.

"As far as that is concerned, what does he mean by '*minimize your losses*,' and who do we '*pay restitution*' to in his scenario of redemption?" Jo-Ellen asked. It sounds like a bunch of rambling from someone high on drugs, Jo-Ellen said.

"Maybe, but maybe not," Jonathan cautioned. "I think we should set up a fund at a local bank, advertise that action in the local newspaper, and see what results, if any, we get from the perp. As long as we don't make anyone in particular a signer on the account, what can it hurt? I'll get that done this afternoon, and we can put a four-line ad in the newspaper saying what we've done."

"How much money should we put in the account?" Maggie asked.

"I have no idea, but I would say a significant amount to show that we are sincere," Jonathan said.

"Are we sincere?" Jo-Ellen asked.

"We're sincere in the fact that we want to catch this crazed perp who goes around threatening to harm people, poisoning folks with arsenic, and who is capable of much more disastrous deeds," Jonathan said.

"I'll agree with that comment. But how do you catch someone who is not rational, and who is so unpredictable?"

"You go fishing," Jonathan said.

"Fishing?" Jo-Ellen asked. "How can fishing help us catch someone like this?"

"I'll tell you what I was told as a young boy when my father took me deep sea fishing off the coast of Boston. There was a trawler that went out every day to fish for all kinds of things that the people of Boston loved to eat from the sea. Flounder, striped bass, and, of course, lobsters were the prize everyone was trying to catch to sell to the food brokers on the docks and to take home and cook for dinner. I was only about nine years old when we went out that summer, and I asked him how you catch this kind of fish, and how you catch that kind of fish. Do you know what he told me?"

"I have no idea, Jonathan," Maggie said.

"He said just use the kind of bait each particular kind of fish you want to catch likes to eat."

"I thought all fish liked worms," Jo-Ellen said.

"That's not necessarily true, but I guess if they're hungry enough they would bite a worm on a hook. Black sea bass are bottom feeders, and they are mostly attracted to mollusks, baitfish, mussels, and squid. Lobsters are usually caught in a pot, a type of cage, and they are mostly attracted to blue fish, cod, and mackerel, but their favorite food is salted herring. And while flounder can be hooked like any other fish, they are more easily gigged with a special rod and reel and cranked into the boat by the fisherman who stands in a deep-well boat, throwing his gig or spear into the shallow water when they are on beds."

"That's a lot to have to know about different kinds of fish to be successful trying to catch one's dinner," Jo-Ellen laughed.

"That's the point, Jo-Ellen. If you're fishing for catfish, you leave your live bait lying on the bottom of the lake or river, because that's where the catfish are to be found. They will eat a lot of different things, but they are not generally going to chase a lure like a bass or a bream. Likewise, when you 'fish' for a crook, you fish a certain way to catch a certain kind of crook. If we think the perp is a megalomaniac, we feed that need which has him believing that he has control and power over everyone around him. If we think the perp we're after is a schizophrenic, we try to feed him information which tends to make his delusions and possible hallucinations more controllable so he will cooperate with us. In other words, we 'fish' with the right bait, and we catch who we are trying to catch."

"All that sounds fine, but how do we know which bait to use on this guy?"

"Right now, we don't, but that can change. We keep him or her talking and communicating with us until we get a break."

"And you think the email will tell us something about the perp?"

"First, we have to ask ourselves why he would write it, and then what he thinks it will accomplish? If we can figure out one or both of those things, we may be able to figure out where his head is in all of this, and then we try to find him physically."

"Your suggestion sounds almost undoable."

"The first thing we know is that if this perp had wanted to kill more people, he surely could have done so. How many casualties do you think we would have had if his goal had been to just cause death?

"I see your point. Do you see his action as a cry for help? That's a rather dramatic way to ask for help if you ask me."

"Jo-Ellen, do you know why arsonists many times come back to the fires that they have started and stand around in the crowd? Or why bank robbers go back to the very banks that they've robbed after they have made clean getaways?"

"I don't have a clue," she said.

"The psychiatrists who have questioned these criminals tell their doctors that it was for a desire for control and power. By setting the fire, they feel that they control the scene where firefighters have to come to the building, rescue the endangered victims, and douse the flames, if possible. The same can be said for the bank robber. It's not that they really want to get caught, as you may have heard some TV analysts parrot over and over, but rather it's a control issue for most of these violent criminals."

"Relating what you just said to our situation, you don't think the person who laced the food or drinks of those who died by ingesting arsenic really wants to get caught, and it's not just a cry for help?"

"No, I think it's much like the bank robber or the arsonist. If you know that you can control what happens to someone's life simply by slipping something in their drink that will kill them, that's ultimate power to a demented mind. It's not a lot different than an aggressive date using a roofie,

Rohypnol, GHB, or Ketamine to induce unconsciousness and loss of memory for a victim who has been attacked by a rapist or molester. He seeks control over his victim, but his motive is sexual satisfaction rather than seeing a building burn to the ground or a bank teller freak when he puts a gun in his or her face. However, the fear is the same, and the motivation is the same. Power over someone else at their expense!" Jo-Ellen thought about it for a few minutes and then suggested that they look for that kind of person, rather than just performing a meaningless search of vendor who may have had nothing at all to do with poisoning the two victims.

"Your idea is great, Jo-Ellen," Maggie said. "How do you propose we go about finding that person in a sea of 250,000 people who are inebriated and eating shrimp by the buckets? They are as thick as ticks on a June bug down on the beach."

"Ticks on a June bug?" Jo-Ellen said with a laugh. "Maggie, you have truly become a Southerner with language like that!" Everyone had a good laugh, but Jo-Ellen had a point. You wouldn't look for a shark in the woods, nor would you look for a reptile in the desert. You look for things in their commonly known place of existence. Defining the kind of place where a potential murderer might hang out could be tricky, but Jo-Ellen doubted that it would be at a soda shop where they served up cosmopolitan ice cream in sugar cones. She just had to consider where someone with those types of ambitions would congregate in Baldwin County.

"Maggie, I think it may be time for us to call in our old friend Larry Pennington," Jonathan said. "What do you think?" Larry Pennington was a profiler whom Jonathan and Maggie had used on a regular basis when they both worked for the city of Rowlette, Illinois, a few years ago. Larry had since retired from full-time work, but he still consulted at times for old friends or for those willing to pay him a tidy fee and all his expenses. Maggie and Jonathan had employed Larry once after they moved to Gulf Shores, flying him in from Chicago, offering to put him up in a nice hotel on the beach, flying him to and from Gulf Shoes on a private jet, and otherwise treating him like the professional he had become. Just having someone analyze the tendencies of a perp, give a set of particulars he created out of thin air from his personal experiences in the past working with certain types of individuals, and type-casting the image of the perp would not necessarily hasten finding who might be trying to get their attention in the National Shrimp Festival case, but it was well worth the try. Jonathan would call Larry Pennington and set things up.

"I think it's time I got out and walked around the beach area one more time," Jo-Ellen said to no one in particular. "Maybe the sea breezes and salty air will jolt my consciousness into a good idea."

"While you do that, Jo-Ellen, I will place a call to our friend in Rowlette and see if he is available. There are other profilers, but I have total trust in Larry's approach to the science of the troubled mind!" Jonathan said with a laugh. Jonathan placed the call on speaker, dialed the number, and waited for Larry to pick up. The call went to voicemail, so Jonathan left the message for Larry to return the call at his earliest convenience. That was all he could do. Within twenty minutes, Jonathan's cell phone rang, he picked up the call, and he heard his familiar friend on the other end of the line.

"Jonathan? This is Larry Pennington. I'm sorry I missed your call, but I was indisposed working on a lead for the Rowlette Police Department. How can I be of help to you?"

"How would you like a distraction and a trip to the beach? Maggie and I could really use your help on a matter down here."

"I'm not really doing anything much which would prevent me from taking you up on your offer. What did you have in mind?" Jonathan explained that they needed a profile on a potential megalomaniac who apparently had poisoned a couple of people to get the attention of those he wished to influence. While it wasn't necessarily a classic signature of a psychotic killer, the acts of this crazed person had all the potential of becoming a serious event, and one which could damage or destroy the National Shrimp Festival for years to come.

"If you remember our arrangements the last time you came and visited with us, we will do the same for you this time. You are welcomed to stay for a couple of weeks, if you prefer, on the beach in a nice hotel, all expenses, and we will charter a private bird to fly you in and back just like we did last time. I think we paid you a $10,000 per diem check for your troubles last time, and this trip will be worth that much to us again if you can work us in quickly. We're concerned that we don't have too much time before the perp strikes again."

"Let me check my calendar, Jonathan," he said, and Larry put down his cell and disappeared from the call momentarily.

"What do you think, Jonathan? Do you think he'll come?" Maggie asked, cupping her hand over the phone sitting on the desk so Larry would not be able to hear her question.

"Yes, and I think he's just trying to convince us that he is staying busy since he retired from active work as a profiler." The phone line was picked up once more and Larry's voice was heard again.

"I cleared my calendar for the next seven days, so I can leave within the hour, if it's an emergency."

"It's definitely something which we need to get done sooner than later. I will put in a call and have a Gulfstream G-7 waiting for you at the local airport in Rowlette within the hour. You will fly into the Jack Edwards National Airport, and if you leave within the hour, you can be here by lunchtime." Everyone agreed, and Jonathan hung up.

"I guess Larry still keeps a 'go-bag' available for emergencies," Maggie said. "Deep down, I think he still loves being needed."

"Most of us don't feel appreciated as much when we retire as you and I do, but we started a meaningful business adventure to help people, and it's kept us busy and has continued to give us a feeling of fulfilment. Larry probably doesn't get called to perform his skill set as much as he did when we were in Rowlette."

"He's a good man, and if he can help us identify and stop this perp who is terrorizing the National Shrimp Festival it will be well worth the expense." Maggie tipped her orange juice glass toward Jonathan, and he returned the gesture with his ceramic coffee cup. Maggie thought how fortunate they were to have unlimited financial assets to use as they needed to help the local government agencies solve these otherwise impossible crimes.

Jo-Ellen had dragged the Murder Board out of the office closet, cleaned the erasers from their earlier use, and made sure she had multiple-colored temporary markers for use in posting their progress as they received clues about the National

Shrimp Festival murderer. Maggie gave Jo-Ellen a thumbs-up signal, and Jonathan suggested that everyone take a little time to compose their personal thoughts about the person or persons who had begun to terrorize 250,000 people on the beach who had done nothing to deserve such treatment. While they waited for Larry Pennington to arrive later in the day, Jo-Ellen could start her list, and they could get some idea of whom they were dealing with who was threatening the annual shrimp festival. Having a world-class profiler was much better than depending on a gypsy reading the tea leaves for clues who was causing such chaos, and everyone hoped that Larry Pennington would be more correct than that a gypsy! It was clear to everyone that Larry's private plane would not reach Gulf Shores by lunchtime, so Jonathan volunteered to walk over to the public beach area and buy some fresh seafood for their lunch. No one disagreed that his idea was a great one, so Jonathan caught the elevator to the main floor, had a fistful of cash in his hand, and was about to leave the parking lot when someone hit him on the back of his head, and everything went dark. The next thing he remembered was waking up in the South Baldwin Medical Center Emergency Room, lying on a gurney, with something being injected into his arm. As his vision cleared, he saw Jo-Ellen, Maggie, and Maria standing by his gurney.

"Am I dying?" he halfway joked.

"Nope, but you're probably going to have one hell of a headache when the swelling goes down on the back of your head and the pain medications wear off," Maggie said. "What do you remember about being attacked?"

"What time is it?" Jonathan asked without answering Maggie's question.

"It's almost 6:00 PM. You evidently lost consciousness when you were attacked, and we didn't know you had been accosted for over an hour. One of the other residents found your body in the parking deck and called 911," Maggie said.

"I guess I was robbed?" he asked.

"Nope, and that's what's so strange about all of this," Jo-Ellen said. "When you were admitted to the ER you had your Rolex on your wrist, your rings on your fingers, and your wallet was untouched. All of your credit cards, driver's license, and cash were still in your wallet. You weren't robbed, but rather assaulted."

"Does anyone have a good idea why?"

"We don't have to wonder, Jonathan. Your attacker left a typewritten note," Maggie said. She showed Jonathan the note, did not read it to him, and put it back in her pocket.

"I forgot about Larry Pennington coming to town. Did someone meet his plane?"

"I did," Jo-Ellen said. "He's resting comfortably at the Best Western Hotel on the beach, and he seems to have no complaints. I told him to enjoy his stay and that we would be in touch with him soon. I didn't tell him about your attack."

"That's probably a good thing. I don't want him to think that he is in danger," Jonathan said.

"We all might be in danger now that the perp has raised his level of violence to attacking us personally," Maggie said. "Are you sure you're going to be alright?"

"I'll be fine. Someone get me released from here so I can get back to work," he demanded.

"Not so fast," Maggie said. "The doctors want you to stay overnight for observation since you had a concussion, and I think it's a good idea."

"Absolutely not," Jonathan said. "We don't have time for me to languish in a comfortable hospital bed while someone is attacking and murdering people for no clear reason. Get me released—now!" Maggie couldn't do anything with Jonathan when he got this way, so she got the nurse to start the paperwork so Jonathan could be released later that evening. "We need to meet with Larry Pennington as soon as I get out of here," he said.

"At least you should rest if you're not going to follow the doctor's advice and stay overnight. Larry can keep until morning," Maggie said.

"That's not wise," Jonathan said, showing that he had a grip on reality once more. "At no minor expense, we flew him to Gulf Shores expeditiously, told him that this was a matter of extreme urgency, and then we let him wonder what's going on for over twelve hours while he sits in a hotel room? Does that make sense?"

"I'm assuming you don't want him to know that you were attacked?" Maggie asked.

"Not just yet. It might help him with his profile once he has worked through the other assumptions and facts we already know about the perp, but right now I don't want to throw other factors into the mix. I want a genuine opinion of who and why someone would poison innocent people without reason, and me being attacked probably had nothing to do with the first act by the perp."

"If that's the way you want this to play out, we will handle it your way. However, I do believe you should report this incident to CPT Phillips as soon as possible. You were assaulted, for whatever reason, and that is something the public should be aware of."

"What did the note say?" Jonathan remembered Maggie showing him the note briefly, and then putting it back in her pocket.

"It doesn't really matter at this time, Jonathan. You need to rest," she demanded.

"It matters to me what the note says, especially since it was my head that was bashed in by the perp." Maggie took the note back out of her pocket and gave it to Jonathan to read.

"Can you read it, or do you need for me to read it to you?"

"You read it to me. My vision is still a little blurred." The note was typed neatly, there were no misspelled words, or any cut-and-paste efforts of Jonathan's attacker to further disguise his identity. The note simply read:

You are wasting my time, and I will not be generous to anyone who wastes my time. I know you opened the bank account like I asked, but you have more to do. Check the history of your own misdeeds! Do it now!

"What do we do with as message like that, Jonathan?" Jo-Ellen asked.

"Honestly, Jo-Ellen, right now I can't give you a good answer. Let's think through this and the first email and see if we can decipher just what the perp is trying to tell us. If one could read tone into a written message or an email, I would have to say he appears to be getting frustrated with the progress we've made toward his demands."

They all decided to let Jonathan get some rest, even though he kept threatening to get up out of the bed and go home. Maggie had spoken to the doctor away from Jonathan's bedside, and she asked him to give Jonathan a mild sedative which would make him tired and drowsy so he would go back to sleep. That's what the doctor did, and Jonathan would never know that Maggie was the reason he didn't really feel like going home that afternoon. It was a win-win for everyone.

Chapter 8
A Persecuted Mind

Arthur Murry had not been happy growing up in South Alabama with the famous name given to him by his parents. They both loved ballroom dancing, and since their last name was Murry, they thought it would be neat to have a son named after the famous ballroom dancer and entrepreneur. Of course, the Arthur Murray who was the professional ballroom dancer spelled his name with an added "a" before the last letter of his name, a fact no one ever seemed to notice or care. The name stuck, and Arthur would eventually believe that the unfortunate event that caused him to be named after the famous clinician caused many of his lifelong problems. Contrary to his namesake, Arthur Murry was a misfit and a loser, according to modern day society values. He was teased throughout grammar school and high school, tried to enlist in the U.S. Army but was disqualified for some vague reason which the government could not fully explain to him. Arthur believed they might have thought that he was gay, and when he was at the age to enlist in the military there was no war on anywhere, and the military could reject anyone for any reason. The fact that Arthur had a lisp and was a little effeminate didn't help his case. Whether or not he was gay had never really crossed his mind until everyone kept trying to stereotype him and put him in that category. He had never had any significant relationships with girls or women, but he just thought it was because he was so awkward and came across as a nerd.

Arthur decided that since everyone treated him as like he was gay, he would receive help from the inclusion of that particular group of people. He went to barber school, learned how to cut and style hair, and decided that he could make a decent living helping people groom themselves for the proper activities which they were interested in doing. He became quite proficient and was sought out by many female and male clients to coif their hair exactly as they wanted.

Growing up in Baldwin County, in the small town of Magnolia Springs, Arthur never really fit in with the boys his age when he was attending school. He was not athletic, and when he tried to play baseball or other sports with his peers he seemed to always get hurt. He broke his arm when he was nine years old, his right leg when he was twelve, and is collarbone when he was fifteen. All incidents came when he was trying to compete in the typical sports boys play when they are teens and young boys. His mother suggested he learn to play chess and try out for the debate team, but most of the kids involved with those activities were loners, much like Arthur. He wanted to break out of his shell and have fun like all the other kids, but it just wasn't to be. What Arthur took away from his experiences was anger and disappointment that he just wasn't good enough to play with his peers on an equal footing.

Arthur held down several meaningless jobs until he got his barber's license and began to cut and style hair. He could put his quiet personality to work at this new job, and he had enough time to begin to work out at the gym in his spare time. Arthur wasn't a scrawny kid, but he wasn't a muscular one either. He had been pushed around by grammar school kids, his high school peers, and most everyone else in his life because he was shy, retiring, and a weakling, according to his own critical analysis of himself. That was going to change.

Arthur began going to the gym three times a week, and he just watched what everybody else did to work out. It wasn't working for him, and he was getting discouraged and almost gave up before one of the trainers noticed how hard Arthur was trying to improve himself. He told Arthur that he would give him free lessons for four weeks, providing that Arthur would work hard and be at the gym on time three days a week. Arthur agreed, and in a matter of just a few weeks he was beginning to feel stronger and more confident in himself. During the last session of the last free week of training, his coach pulled him aside and asked him if he wanted to continue to work with him.

"Absolutely," Arthur gushed. "This is the best thing I've ever done for myself!"

"Arthur, do you mind if I ask you a personal question?"

"Sure, what is it?"

"Are you gay?" The question caught Arthur off guard, and he almost dropped the dumbbell he had been holding. "I don't mean to pry into your personal affairs, and you don't have to tell me, but I've just noticed a few things that made me wonder about you."

"To be totally honest with you, I don't know. I'm not particularly attracted to men or to women, but I've never hooked up with a man before. You aren't asking me out, are you?" His coach laughed.

"No, Arthur. I'm straight, but it doesn't matter to me if you're straight, guy, or bi-sexual. I'm only interested in helping you reach the level of muscle tone and fitness you wish to achieve."

"Then why did you ask if I were gay? Was it my mannerisms?" The coach laughed once more.

"No. What I have discovered over the many years that I have been working with individuals who want to improve their body strength and stamina is that gay people usually tend to hold back some, and they don't push themselves as far as they are capable many times during a workout. This can result in less than desired results, and disappointment overall with their coach or trainer. That's why I was curious."

"Am I slacking off? Do I need to push harder?"

"How do you feel about those two questions?"

"I could do more. I just need someone to stay on my butt and make me do things right."

"That's a job that I can do, Arthur. Let's get back to our workout schedule. I do this for a living, so I am here five days a week from 7:00 AM until 6:00 PM. You need to find an hour three days a week when you can match my schedule, and let's plan a six-month program to get you into tip-top physical shape. Does that work for you?"

"Sure. What do you charge for your instruction?"

"I normally charge $100 per hour for individual sessions, but it you commit to the six-month program, I'll only charge you $1000 per month, which saves you about 25% of the overall fee. If after a month you decide that you need to cut back or even drop out of the program, that's okay. This is something that you will be doing for your own self-esteem, and for no one else."

"I'm in, Leon. What days' work for you? I'll plan my days around your schedule. I am my own boss, and I can make my own schedule." They synchronized their schedules and came up with a plan for Arthur to train with Leon three times a week for the next six months. The decision to gain control of his personal life was a turning point for Arthur Murry.

Leon Douglas was a successful businessman turned athletic coach in his later years after making a small fortune in the stock market. All those years while he was dressing in his three-piece suit, driving to downtown Mobile to work in a high-rise bank building, Leon wanted to do what he had dreamed of doing when he was growing up in the slums of the city of Mobile. One of his heroes growing up had been Muhammed Ali, and Leon had followed his training routine on his off time to try and stay in shape himself. It was difficult, with late evening client dinners, business trips away from home for weeks at a time, and a family of three, a wife and two kids, to take care of as well. Leon had to work at something which would yield an opportunity for him to take care of his family financially, and he hit the jackpot when he got involved in trading stocks and bonds. In just three years he had become a millionaire several times over, and he could now pursue his great love—physical fitness. He started volunteering at the gym, and then was hired by a couple of his big-time stock trading friends to help them get in shape. Leon attributed their interest in physical fitness due to both of them having mid-life crises, but all Leon cared about was helping them achieve their physical fitness goals. Now, after five years at the gym, Leon had built himself a nice business of strength and fitness coaching, and he was getting paid to do what he really loved.

Leon felt constrained at the local gym with his clients, so he bought an old warehouse which was still in pretty good shape, and he remodeled it to make it his private space for coaching weightlifting and physical fitness exercises. It was located just off the public beach in Gulf Shores, had adequate parking, and was within walking distance of a track where Leon's students could log laps around a public parking lot that connected with the beachfront. It was perfect. Arthur had been training at Leon's gym for three years now, and he had totally remade his body from a weakling to a man with six-pack abs, biceps and triceps that were noticeable even through a long-sleeved shirt, and an eighteen-inch neck which wasn't fat. All that came crashing down when Leon come in one day and told everyone that he would be shutting down the gym at the end of the week. He wouldn't elaborate on the reasons why the gym was closing, but Leon had had enough with the city, and he decided to just close his business altogether. It was a sad day for everyone involved.

Arthur joined another gym, but it was never quite the same as when Leon had his private gym. There was someone present at all times to help spot the weightlifters, and they did give some free advice, but it was just not the same without Leon. And then two things happened which made Arthur angry and for which he could not forgive. The city had condemned the old gym even though Leon had made major repairs to ensure that it was a safe environment, and he and his entire company were evicted and moved out in record time. To further discourage those involved with the gym situation, a report was published which said that the building would be demolished, and the land would be repurposed for the betterment of the neighborhood. The final insult to Leon and those who had been loyal to his gym and commitment to the community, a fire mysteriously broke out in the gym while Leon was pursuing legal action against the city reducing the once historic building to nothing but ashes. Leon had been sleeping in the gym to protect it against looters who anticipated the wrecking ball's work at any time, and he was tragically killed in the fire, leaving a wife, two small children, and many patrons heartsick at the ramifications of what they saw as pure greed on the part of the city to increase the tax base with new construction where the gym had stood for almost 100 years, providing recreational opportunities to the community at large. Accusations flew back and forth as to whom was the firebug, but arson could not be proven, and the memory of Leon and his efforts just faded into the past. All that happened almost ten years ago, but there was still enmity between the city and those most directly affected by the city's desire to gentrify the old gym and its surrounding land. Arthur Murry took the tragic sequence of events harder than most of Leon's other devotees. Arthur had attributed Leon to virtually saving his life, and now his savior had been sacrificed on the altar of greed and avarice.

In a twist of fate for Arthur, Leon had actually left some money in his will for Arthur, with the caveat that Arthur continues to fight the good fight for the downtrodden and underappreciated citizens of Baldwin County and the city of Gulf Shores. Leon left a trust fund to be used exclusively for helping others like Arthur had once been, and he made Arthur the executor of that fund. Knowing that it could develop into a full-time job for Arthur, Leon supplied more than enough cash for Arthur to live on for the rest of his life, assuming he continued to support and encourage Leon's ideals throughout the Baldwin County area. And although the guidelines for Leon's idea of perpetual care for the homeless and those thrown away by today's society were broad, Leon left Arthur as the sole person to decide the actions to be taken to help those in need. Arthur assumed the responsibility of the herculean task and he continued the good fight against those preferring progress over compassion.

* * *

It had been almost ten years since Leon had sacrificed himself as one who wanted the best possible lifestyle for all of the citizens of Baldwin County. In the place where the old gym had been now stood an eighteen-story condominium named the Crown Victoria Condominiums, a tribute to the rich and famous, or at least that's how Leon had imagined why it had been constructed. As far as Arthur was concerned, one was either part of the solution or part of a continuing problem. When Arthur did his research on the construction of the Crown Victoria Condominium complex and the investors involved, a billionaire who was moving from the Chicago area was putting up the funding for the new construction, and he had had the audacity to buy the entire top floor of the condominium building as his private residence and office complex. Although legal in every way, the immorality of replacing Leon's vision of helping those less fortunate with an eyesore which towered above the sacred land where Leon had died in the fire was just too much for Arthur to digest. He turned his attention to getting justice and honor for Leon's memory. These people would pay, and would pay dearly, for what they had done.

Leon Douglas' wife and children had moved on with their lives. His wife had not remarried, and she was able to support her two children in the lifestyle in which they had been provided while their father was still alive since Leon had left each of them trust funds to pay for their basic needs and future educational opportunities. They had grown up, gone to college, and moved away from Gulf Shores. Leon's wife also moved elsewhere, but no one ever heard where she had gone after the fire and Leon's untimely death.

There was no one left in the Gulf Shores area to mourn for Leon and all he had done for the community and the downtrodden, except for Arthur Murry. Leon had literally changed his life, and Arthur decided to dedicate the remaining years of his life to earn the respect of his long-long mentor and friend by righting the wrongs done to him and his dream by the city of Gulf Shores and the rich tycoon who had displaced all their lives. Granted it had been ten years since Leon's death and the scattering of his dreams, but Arthur Murry had not lost focus over the past decade to do something dramatic to revere his good friend and savior Leon Douglas.

Chapter 9
Larry Pennington's Profile

While Maggie had tricked Jonathan into taking medication which would cause him to continue to be drowsy and feel less than ready to resume his duties at M&J Investigations, she knew that it was for his own good, and she had no regrets for taking that action. What she loved most about her fiancé was his unstoppable energy and focus when he decided something needed to be done, but Maggie also dreaded it when Jonathan was acting like a dog chasing a squirrel. All her young life as a girl growing up in Rowlette, Illinois, was spent living outside the city limits of town in a mostly rural community. She had a wonderful hairy friend, Scotty, a wire-haired terrier, who chased squirrels in the yard every single day of his existence, never even getting close to catching one. She would sit Scotty down on her knee, look deeply into his chocolate brown eyes, and try to explain to him the physiology of squirrels and canines, and that Scotty could never outrun, out weave, or outclimb a squirrel. He looked back into Maggie's eyes with the confidence that he knew what he was doing, and that she should mind her own business, or that's what Maggie thought Scotty might be saying. As soon as she put Scotty back down on the ground, he would tear out again after one of the many squirrels who tortured him daily with their antics.

That's why Jonathan frustrated her. He was like Scotty. He was loyal, loved Maggie with all his being, but just couldn't get it through his thick skull when she was trying to convince him to do good things for himself, like resting one more day after being plunked on the head by a perp. He was so much like her Scotty when she was a girl in Rowlette. Today Jonathan was back at work in a limited capacity, refusing to take muscle relaxers and other drugs which could have made his physical pain less present, but which also continued to cause him to lose clarity when he tried to think about finding and catching the perp who not only plunked him on the head, but possibly murdered two innocent people just to get their attention. Jonathan was sitting on the balcony, sipping a cup of hot, black coffee Maria had made for the office, and looking at the perpetual crashing of the waves of the Gulf of Mexico eighteen stories beneath his feet. Maggie had retrieved a cup of coffee from the kitchen and had pulled up a wicker chair next to Jonathan's on the balcony.

"Good morning, Jonathan," she said and reached down to give him a tender kiss on the forehead. "I'm glad you are feeling better today." Jonathan had suspected that Maggie had encouraged the ER doctor to give Jonathan medication to incapacitate him for another day and keep him in the hospital overnight, but Jonathan would never verbalize such an accusation. Lt.

Maggie Watson could be fierce in her defense of a loved one, event to the extent of altering their medications for their own good, but actually calling her out on such charges was never a good idea!

"I'm going to be fine. Did Larry Pennington get settled into his hotel room comfortably last night?"

"Larry is doing just fine, and there have been no complaints from him about his accommodations or his beneficial treatment at the hands of the Best Western concierge and the services given to him since he has been their guest. I called him earlier this morning and told him as soon as you are feeling up to it today that we would send Maria for him. You, me, Jo-Ellen, and Larry will put our heads together and come up with some kind of profile to work on trying to find who is causing all of this grief to the National Shrimp Festival and why he's doing it."

"Give me an hour to get a shower, dress, and compose myself, and then send for Larry. I don't want to waste another day of the National Shrimp Festival knowing the perp may strike again." Maggie agreed, had Maria call Larry at the hotel and inform him that she would be by to pick him up in about an hour, and then Maggie oversaw Jonathan's preparation for the day. The last thing she wanted was for him to get woozy again, fall in the shower, and hit his head. She could be motherly at times, at least when she really needed to be. True to his word, one hour later Jonathan was dressed, sitting at one of the computers in the office, and preparing for their visit with Larry Pennington. Maria collected Larry from the Best Western on the beach, and they all were putting their heads together in the sitting area of M&J Investigation's office.

"Jonathan, are you feeling better?" Larry asked his most gracious host.

"I'm fine. Just got a little bump on the head, spent some time in the ER yesterday, but I'm as good as new today," Jonathan boasted. Maggie rolled her eyes at Jo-Ellen, but fortunately she was sitting behind Larry so he couldn't see her frustration with her fiancé.

"Where did you want me to start with the perp you want a profile on? I looked at the material that Maria brought by the hotel last evening, including the personal attack on you, and I wish I had a better prognosis for your situation." That was an ominous opening, even for a profiler.

"You make it sound pretty dire, Larry. Where are you picking up on that vibe?"

"Knowing Jonathan, as I have learned about him over the years, he travels with a gold Rolex watch, 24-carat gold rings, usually a couple of thousands of cash in his wallet, along with many credit and debit cards, to include a black American Express Centurion Card with unlimited daily withdrawal limits. All in all, I would say the perp could have made himself $100,000 richer with little or no effort by simply robbing Jonathan in the parking lot. However, he took the other route, to threaten him and everyone associated with the National Shrimp Festival if they didn't follow some yet-to-be-defined rules which he plans to share soon with you all. He apparently knows who Jonathan is now, and I doubt the attack was random. It appears to be more personal in nature, and that makes it more dangerous to all of you, and to Jonathan in particular."

"You're just full of good news, aren't you?" Jonathan teased Larry.

"You said you wanted the truth, but in remembrance of the famous line from 'A Few Good Men,' can you *handle* the truth? The truth is that you have an unusual person or persons gunning for you, possibly your team, and possibly either the National Shrimp Festival or the city of Gulf Shores. I'm not sure which one is most applicable at this time."

"What about the murders? How do they tie into all of this?"

"I hate to burst your bubble, but I'm not sure that the same person who attacked Jonathan is the one who poisoned the festival attendees. You may have multiple dynamics going on here." Maggie looked at Jo-Ellen and Jonathan and just sighed. This case was getting complicated.

"Help me out here, Larry. Are you saying we have two different murderers or attackers working the National Shrimp Festival?" Jonathan asked.

"I can't tell you that, but I can tell you this much. The person who attacked you wasn't a murderer, or at least he wasn't the day he decided to plunk you on the head. You were as vulnerable as you will ever be when attacked from behind by an unseen assailant, and he could surely have snuffed out your life as easily as snuffing out a candle at the altar. So, what you really need to know is why the particular perp who attacked you did not take your life, if he is the same person who poisoned the people at the shrimp festival. Logic says that he isn't the same person."

"That's just swell," Jonathan groused. "Do we come up with two separate profiles now? One for the murderer and one for my attacker?"

"I'm just not sure right now, and here's why. The murderer could be your attacker, but your attacker is probably not the murderer. Does that make sense to you?"

"Not a word of it," Jonathan said appearing very frustrated with this favorite profiler. "I'm accepting what you're saying because over the years you have been dead-on with your profiles almost 100% of the time. We just need some help with both of these people, assuming we're dealing with two different sets of perps."

"What do you suggest Larry? How do we move forward and keep a watchful eye on these perps at the same time?" Maggie asked.

"I rarely ever give this kind of advice, because I'm not a detective nor do I think like one of you mysterious people," he said with a chuckle, "but you might consider confronting the perp who struck you on the head to determine what his real beef is with you personally. Once you know his complaint, you can decide whether or not to address it formally."

"Isn't that dangerous?"

"Probably, but otherwise he may attack you again, and the outcome could be much worse. If you sustain too many head traumas, you can have permanent brain damage."

"What I don't understand is that both messages sent to us refer to us 'doing the right thing,' so how can they be from different sources?"

"I can't answer that question for you, other than saying there may be two factions working within the organization with the perp who attacked you. I would be most surprised if the same person who attacked you poisoned anyone. That's my professional opinion. Take it or leave it."

Jonathan thanked Larry, told him that he could stay at the Best Western Hotel as long as he liked, and that M&J Investigations would fly him home the same way they flew him down to Gulf Shores whenever he was ready to return to the Chicago area. He thanked Larry for his analysis and gave him a nice bonus over and above the stipend he had promised him when he spoke to him on the phone. Larry thanked Jonathan for his continued generosity and told him that he was sorry he couldn't give him the kind of report he was hoping for, but that he really felt strongly about his analysis and profile on the person who had attacked Jonathan. Maria escorted Larry back to the hotel, and Jonathan, Maggie, and Jo-Ellen went to the balcony overlooking the beach to discuss Larry's results.

"Well, what do you think, Maggie?" Jonathan asked his beautiful fiancée.

"Do I think Larry is correct with his profile of our murderer? Or do I think his profile is nearer to being correct for the perp who clunked you on the head? Which question should I answer?"

"Does that mean you think there are two different groups of people trying to upset and do damage to the National Shrimp Festival?"

"One reason we have always had so much confidence in Larry Pennington is that he is so often correct in his assumptions. Maybe we ought to ask ourselves if we are doubting his profile because we don't like what he has told us, and not that it may be totally incorrect. Let's look back over the message the perp left you when he personally attacked you." Maggie went into the office, printed out the message in three copies, and brought them all a copy of their last communication with the perp. Maggie read the message aloud while Jonathan and Jo-Ellen listened for clues to what the perp was trying to say.

"You are wasting my time, and I will not be generous to anyone who wastes my time. I know you opened the bank account like I asked, but you have more to do. Check the history of your own misdeeds! Do it now!"

"Jonathan, it's obvious to me that he is directing this note to you, not to the city of Gulf Shores or the National Shrimp Festival organizers."

"How can that be? We haven't been here long enough to have any history this perp can dispute, have we?"

"Since we are detectives, let's detect!" Maggie said. "What have we done since we got to Gulf Shores?"

"We set up an organization to help small governments deal with hard to solve crimes. How can that offend anyone whom we would care about?"

"I don't think that's it," Jo-Ellen said. "What else did you do when you were getting setup in Gulf Shores?"

"Nothing that I can put my finger on. Can you remember anything that we did which might have offended someone, Maggie?" She thought for a moment and just shook her head.

"All we did was find a place to live, buy into his condominium in which we now live, and move in once it was completed. The project was well underway before I got involved financially in it and altered the project to meet our personal and business needs. How could that possibly offend, and *who* could it offend?"

"I don't know, Jonathan, but reading this message from the perp who beaned you on the head, you and the construction team must have done something to piss someone off pretty bad. I'm looking at this from the outside, and you and Maggie are looking at things from a different perspective."

"Okay, Jo-Ellen, you have convinced me. It has something to do with me or this building we are not working out of. Maybe the perp wants us to go back to the beginning and the roots of the construction of the Crown Victoria Condominiums. It's now your job, Jo-Ellen, to find the reason the perp is pissed off. Do you think you can do that for us?"

"Your wish is my command," Jo-Ellen said, gave a small salute to Jonathan, and headed inside to her computer. Jo-Ellen was good on the computer, and when she was called away into the field when on a case, Maria could pick up where Jo-Ellen left off on her research and never miss a beat. Maggie had walked back into the office as well, and asked Jo-Ellen how she was going to approach her research.

"I wouldn't know where to start on something like that," Maggie said. Do you have any inspirations that tell you how to start your background search?"

"If we take the perp's own words as fact, something that happened years ago upset his applecart, and that's where we need to start. Did someone get beaten out of their property, was the city of Gulf Shores too aggressive in their desire to continue to develop the beach areas around the public beach which has been open to the general public for many years, and now they were planning to restrict its use. Things like that get locals in an uproar, and those feelings can get blown out of proportion quickly." Jo-Ellen asked Maria to see if the city's public land use history was available, and also how zoning may have been changed by the city of Gulf Shores to enhance their opportunity to create more revenue on the valuable land in and around the public beach. Maria would probably need to make a physical visit to the public library to see those articles referring to what was happening ten to twenty years ago, but she had worked in a public library for most of her adult life, so she knew her way around those types of records better than most. Jo-Ellen would go to the city hall itself and see if she could research the permits taken out for construction in the past ten years on or near the beach, and if there were any complications with any of the permitting by the contractors.

When Jo-Ellen visited the city hall she was directed to the Office of Development and

Commerce, which was a new office just created a few years ago as the construction and interest in Gulf Shores had erupted like a volcano. The woman at the desk was friendly, and she showed Jo-Ellen where she could look at the public records of all the permits and construction contracts allowed in the city limits of Gulf Shores. Jo-Ellen spent an hour perusing the records for the land purchases, condominium permits granted by the Development Office of Baldwin County, and any controversial projects that had to be filed more than once because of protests, revocations, or disputes with the local population. Over a span of ten years the number of permits, construction projects, and completed structures were almost too many to count. What did stand out was one particular permitting process for a high-rise condominium right off the public beach. It was the Crown Victoria Condominiums, the very ones which Jonathan and Maggie had converted the top floor to as their home and new office. According to the city's elaborate records, the builder had to work very hard to even get the city to grant him a permit to research constructing the condominium. The timeline for most buildings like the Crown Victoria Condominiums was two years, from the original submitted permit to the zoning department, the special review committee to ensure that the project fell within the parameters of what was considered acceptable and tasteful construction, the letting of the different phases of construction upon the completion of the previous phase, and the final inspections and certificate of occupation, which alone could take three or four months' time to please the municipal authorities overseeing the construction. In the case of the Crown Victoria Condominiums, the total project took four years to complete, and until Jonathan Pembroke put his considerable resources behind the work everything seemed stuck in a political and administrative logjam. A donation here, a letter of financial support there, and the project moved forward quickly. Although Jonathan was discreet in his financial support of the city leaders and their political campaigns, there was still a public record of his involvement in the project. Jo-Ellen made a note of these transactions and texted Maria to search in the stacks for any newspaper story which might correspond to the project. Having discovered a possible smoking gun for some hard feelings by some local folks, Jo-Ellen headed back to the office. Maria texted Jo-Ellen and told her that there was a huge story about six years ago concerning the construction of the condominium complex now known as the Crown Victoria Condominiums. She told Jo-Ellen that the librarian was kind enough to make copies of the newspaper articles detailing all of the protests and picketing that went on when the previous historic building had been razed to make way for the new condominiums. She said that she was leaving the library and would meet Jo-Ellen at the office, and that they could put their material together before they showed it to Jonathan and Maggie.

Chapter 10
Running the Gauntlet

When a person is attacked, severely criticized, and challenged to a fight, they are often said to be "running the gauntlet," as accused persons had to do in ancient times, running between two rows of people with clubs and sticks to beat them with. It was time for those who had the position of privilege to have to run the gauntlet to receive their just punishment for abusing the rights of others, and Arthur Murry was going to make that happened for those who profited unfairly from the government's takeover of the sacred land where the gym had existed on the beach at Gulf Shores. In Arthur's opinion, it was bad enough for the city to want to profit from a commercial building which would block the vistas from the highway of the beautiful Gulf of Mexico with its sugary sandy beaches, the pounding waves breaking upon the shore, and the oft gorgeous sunsets as the giant orb seemed to sink into the water and get gobbled up by the timeless view of the horizon to the west. Then, if that weren't enough insult to the area, they basically condemned the property where the old gym had been, devastating the dreams of one man who had wanted to make things better for everyone in Gulf Shores. With Leon Douglas, the owner of the gym, dying in a suspicious fire in the condemned building, Arthur had his mission established in his mind. He would fight for the memory of Leon Douglas and all the good which he had done, and was planning to do in the future, for the poor and indigent people in Gulf Shores. Arthur had two options in his mind how to fight the terrible incursion into the private affairs of an individual by big city government. One was to come out in public as to the horrible decision the city fathers had made to seize Leon's property for the better good of the community, or to work from the shadows like he had finally chosen to do. Arthur thought of himself as a possible guerilla soldier, striking his enemy and causing damage, and then disappearing back into the shadows to fight another day. Also, Arthur had no idea how much interest and concern remained in the city after the years had gone by with no one coming to the aid of Leon Douglas' memory and helping to carry on his dream. He might only be one, but Arthur Murry would continue to fight for Leon, even if Leon were no longer around to approve or disapprove of Arthur's actions.

What was a fair response and punishment for those who had crushed Leon's dreams, dashed his hopes for uniting the community through his gym, and wanting to build a better life for his friends and community citizens? Arthur wasn't sure, but he imagined the millions of dollars of commerce which the developer had earned by overtaking Leon's old location, building a multi-million-dollar condominium to be sold to the highest bidder, and blocking out the natural view everyone was entitled to see until the behemoth of an eighteen-story building was constructed on the beach lot which once used to be the gym. Money was the universal language of investors and the greedy but rectifying all the wrong done at the public beach in Gulf Shores would also require a blood sacrifice. *"An eye for an eye, a tooth for a tooth, and a life for a life,"* according to the *Old Testament* Law of Moses, was the payment to be made when such offenses were clear and provable. How many lives had Leon Douglas saved with his gym? It was impossible to know, but Arthur Murry would know when the scales of life were balanced. Not being a very religious man himself, he could only think back to the things he learned at his mother's knee about God's justice and making things right again. Arthur believed in what he was doing now, and he would see things through to the end, even if it cost him his own life.

Arthur had discovered that a major real estate investor from somewhere up north had moved to Gulf Shores several years ago, helped a struggling construction company finish the condominium building now known as the Crown Victoria Condominiums, and had bought the entire top floor for his residence and business offices. There had been hope that the struggling company might not be able to finish the planned construction before this Yankee meddled into the affairs of Gulf Shores and gave them financial stability. Arthur had been following all of the news accounts of this newly planned housing facility, hoping against hope that the city would change its mind, and once again a facility to help all of the people of Gulf Shores could be built where the gym had tragically burned down years ago. But it was not meant to be, and now this huge eyesore of a building was not going anywhere. Arthur had thought of sabotaging it during its construction to discourage the builders from completing it, but he had heard the investor from Illinois had enough money that he would simply start over and continue work until the job was done. So, now Arthur had to exact his revenge and financial payment form the city and from the events the city used to earn revenue on the beach. Arthur wasn't sure what Leon would think of his plans, but he hoped he would be proud of Arthur's singularity of purpose to make the city pay for the injustices of old.

While Arthur had not intended for the two innocents to die when they ingested the arsenic-laced shrimp, he had considered them collateral damage in is war to make things right. There was always collateral damage in a war, wasn't there? These two souls would be only the first of many who paid the price for the city's abject attitude for making things right in the memory of Leon Douglas. How he had managed to sprinkle the two people's shrimp without contaminating others around them was damn near a perfect task carried out. The sleight of hand was what made it work. Arthur had practiced some magic tricks when he was a young man and even put on magic shows for his fellow classmates at times. Unless Arthur explained to those who were investigating how the two people were poisoned and no one else affected, they would never figure it out. There was no smoking gun, and no contaminated dishes or utensils. Just a little fairy-dust which Arthur had figured how to get into the two victim's food. However, now it seemed as if the city was willing to let them be martyrs for the sins of the city planners and employees of city hall. It was time for round two of discreet actions to raise alarm among those beachgoers who financed the city of Gulf Shores and brought in the unimaginable amount of revenue each summer. The tainted shrimp was clever, but it was time to do something much more spectacular to get the city's attention and to show them that Arthur meant business and that his threats were not just idle chatter. But what could Arthur do which would raise even more havoc for the city?

Arnold had made friends with an individual who owned a petting zoo, complete with snakes, large turtles, alligators, and mid-sized sharks. His friend had confessed to Arnold a few weeks before that he could no longer afford to feed and keep the live animals in his care, and he was going to turn them loose in the wild to fend for themselves. He would return back home to the mountains of North

Carolina once the petting zoo was closed and the animals were released. Arnold asked his friend to wait a couple of weeks to release the animals, and he promised to give the owner some funds to help him get readjusted when he returned home to the Carolinas. Since the arsenic scare was not sufficient to get the city of Gulf Shores to act responsibly, Arthur would put plan two into action soon. The petting zoo had boa constrictors, allegators, wild boars, and sharks. The sharks were only about three feet in length, but their fins were large and scary, and Arthur was more into scaring folks than actually harming them. His next act of hostility towards the city of Gulf Shores would be memorable and impressive.

* * *

Jonathan and Maggie had spent some time on the beach, taking in the shrimp stations, visiting the tents authorized by the city of Gulf Shores for the sale of cooked shrimp. Fresh shrimp cocktail was also allowed, but that shrimp had to have been boiled before they could be sold to the public. As a precaution after the scare of those two poisoned with the arsenic laden shrimp earlier in the week, the local health department was keeping a close watch on the preparation and storage of the available shrimp to be bought by the general public.

"I doubt whoever pulled that stunt with the arsenic will try something like that again," Maggie said.

"Do you think he tried to murder more people and just failed in his execution?" Jonathan asked.

"Nope. I think he did exactly what he had planned to do, got the bang for his buck, and is now moving on to another way to disrupt the shrimp festival." Jonathan gave Maggie a questionable look, and then went back to eating boiled shrimp with cocktail sauce.

"What kind of thing do you look for him to pull?"

"Something no one would anticipate," Maggie said.

"Why?"

"Why what?" Maggie asked.

"If this guy is carrying some vendetta against the city of Gulf Shores, why not just poison hundreds of people and get it over with?"

"Jonathan, you are making the classic mistake of judging the motive of the perp by a singular act rather than considering everything else connected with the perp."

"Okay, I confess. I have no idea why he would only kill a couple of folks when he could have made a much bigger statement by killing hundreds. Now, explain to me why you think he purposely killed only two people and not more?"

"I'm not a mind reader, but I would say he was trying to get someone's attention, rather than trying to show that person that he had the power to kill hundreds of people at one time. Actually, he probably made more progress getting whomever attention he was aiming for by only killing two people with one of the most poisonous substances on Earth. It's like he's saying to his target, 'I can kill one or one hundred people, depending on your response to my demands.' Now, whether or not his ploy works is yet to be decided. I would be willing to bet you that he is planning another attack on the city of Gulf Shores, and it will probably be flashier and more dynamic than the taking of two lives with arsenic."

"If you really believe what you're saying, we need to figure out who this guy is and what his next move will be. We should be better detectives than just ones who try to diagnose the results of crimes, and not intervening and preventing them." Maggie was laughing at Jonathan's suggestion, and it make him angry.

"Look, Jonathan. We are neither clairvoyant nor are we fortune tellers. We employ deductive reasoning after a crime is committed to decide who did it, and how they did it. There's nothing mystical about what we do, even if we do it well. I'm just saying if I were the perp, I would do something totally different and outrageous to call attention to my demands. I hope I'm wrong and that this is a one-time event, however, I doubt that's the case. Let's drive to the police station and speak to CPT Phillips and get his take on things. He may have a completely different idea of what is coming." Jonathan agreed, and they got into Maggie's Crown Vic and roared out of the parking lot of the Crown Victoria Condominiums and up Highway 59 North as if it were the Talladega Speedway.

As usual, when Maggie and Jonathan arrived at their favorite police precinct, Maggie parked out front in one of the "For Official Business" parking spots. They got out of the car and went into the lobby area to call on the captain. They were surprised when the desk sergeant told them that the captain had left the comfort of his office and was making a house call.

"Wait. He's making a house call?" Maggie repeated. "When did the Chief of Police begin making house calls? Isn't that what he has patrolmen and underlings for?"

"This is no ordinary house call. It appears that a twenty-seven-foot boa constrictor was trying to eat the resident's poodle, and she wasn't too happy about it." The sergeant raised her eyebrows dramatically to deliver the full effect of the surprise comment.

"Where did this happen?"

"Believe it or not, right in the downtown area of Gulf Shores, out on Highway 59 North. The homeowner called in a panic not knowing if it were legal to kill a boa constrictor, and, if so, how she might go about it. So, the Chief just drove out there to settle things down a bit."

"I can see why the captain might want to get a 'hands-on' account of that complaint before things got out of control."

"To further complicate matters, the homeowner made another call after she called here," the sergeant said with a sigh.

"She called the newspaper?"

"Worse. She called and reported it to the local television station. The film crew was standing there when the captain arrived, began peppering him with all manner of questions, and managed to get an unfriendly response from CPT Phillips. The clip has been playing on the local news station for an hour. It's the NBC News affiliate here in town, so I'm afraid the story will make the national news as well, making a laughingstock of the city of Gulf Shores and CPT Phillips. It's fair to say that he is not the least bit amused." Maggie and Jonathan got the address if of the complainant, got back into her Crown Vic, and they roared off toward the location where the chief was last reportedly seen.

When Maggie and Jonathan pulled up in front of the house where the snake had been reportedly found, Maggie had to stifle a laugh. There was an animal control truck run by the city of Gulf Shores, two police cruisers, and the chief's SUV, all sitting in front of this small bungalow, their red and blue lights blazing like it was the fourth of July. Just then it dawned on Maggie what was probably happening before her eyes.

The perp had unleashed this huge snake upon the good citizens of Gulf Shores, and the chief had to deal with it. Much to the dismay and displeasure of CPT Phillips, the homeowner had also notified the television stations about the rare appearance of a mammoth boa constrictor on the loose in South Alabama, so there would be news reports for days to come on the oddity. What the captain was afraid of was that the perp would get exactly what he had wanted all along from this little prank—24/7 news reports which could be picked up by the local station's national office and broadcast all over the world. Making Gulf Shores the laughingstock and butt of many jokes was not why the city paid their top law enforcement officer. He was there to enforce the law and generate respect throughout the community, and to discourage any display of disrespect to the city and its leaders. So far, CPT Phillips was not succeeding in his mission to do what the council probably thought that they were paying him for. Maggie still saw the humor in the whole affair, even though she would not express those feelings to the police chief. As the monstrous snake was being loaded into the animal control vehicle, CPT Phillips stood quietly with his arms folded across his chest, and not smiling or speaking a word.

"What are the odds a boa constrictor the length of two minivans would show up out of the blue and begin terrorizing my city's citizens?" he asked no one in particular. Jonathan was standing close to him and felt compelled to answer the question posed by the head man in the Gulf Shores Police Department.

"I'd say the odds were pretty good that such a thing *would* happen, Captain." Not believing what he had just heard, Phillips asked Jonathan to clarify what he meant.

"CPT Phillips, Maggie and I think that your city of Gulf Shores is under attack by someone with a vendetta against the city, or at least against someone in city government." The chief looked incredulously at Jonathan seeking a better understanding of his last statement.

"We are a simple, sleepy town on one of the Gulf of Mexico's beaches. Who could have a serious enough beef with us to try to murder people with arsenic or have someone eaten by a gigantic snake? It doesn't add up."

"Are you aware that the city business office has been receiving threats recently about a misjustice done to one of your loyal citizens in the name of profit and greed?" Maggie asked. The chief looked a bit surprised, but nothing really jolted him these days.

"I had heard a rumor that the poisoning of those two beachgoers was tied to some outlandish threat made by an angry local who resented the modernization of the beach areas. In fact, I heard he was pissed about the Crown Victoria Condominium complex that you and Jonathan helped finance. Do you worry about him coming after you and Jonathan?"

"We heard the same thing, but now we believe he has moved on and is behind this boa constrictor stunt."

"And he thinks one big no-poisonous snake is going to bring the city of Gulf Shores to its knees? What a dreamer," the captain said and chuckled.

"We don't know if there are more animals involved at this time, Captain. According to the animal control unit, there are other wild beasts missing from the petting zoo that had made a statement a while ago that they were closing their doors since they could no longer afford to feed their captive animals." Now the police chief didn't think things were so funny, and he unconsciously placed his hand on his Glock.

"I guess we should get a list of all of the animals that were being held in captivity and consider notifying the public about the personal danger to anyone who might come in contact with the beasts."

"We are way ahead of you, Captain," Jonathan smiled and presented an itemized list of live animals which they considered were probably on the loose. The captain read the list out loud, cringing every time he came to an animal that he feared might harm someone.

"Whoever is creating this chaos is not going to get the results he wishes by unleashing wild animals onto the city streets. We will find out who is behind this and stop them in their tracks!" CPT Phillips said.

"How do you plan to do that?" Jonathan asked. "So far, the perp has managed to outwit the entire police department of Gulf Shores, generated public awareness and publicity when he wants it, and is openly mocking anyone having anything to do with the city of Gulf Shores. It sounds like a pretty big task, if you ask me."

"That's why I am asking M&J Investigations to take over and bring this nuisance to a close. We obviously don't have the manpower to chase every lead where an animal appears to be where it's not supposed to be, or to protect every person who fears for his life. Will you and Maggie undertake the job?" Maggie looked at Jonathan and nodded her approval, so Jonathan committed them to solving the murders at the Shrimp Festival, and all the other oddities that had arisen since the poisoning of the two innocents.

"There's only one condition, Captain, that we must demand if we are going to take the lead on this investigation," Maggie said. Looking at her suspiciously, the captain asked what that condition might be. "The person or persons committing these crimes thinks he is acting in the best interests of the people of Gulf Shores."

"In other words, he's deranged?"

"Maybe," Jonathan said. "I think what Maggie is saying is that if you go after this guy like any other perp, you'll miss the subtle messages he's trying to send to you and the city council. Whether he's mentally unstable or not, he believes in his purpose, and that creates a much harder task for us, or for anyone trying to stop him from his ultimate goal."

"And just what is his ultimate goal?" the captain asked.

"When we figure that out, we will be well on our way to figuring out who is causing all this grief and why he's doing it. I have an idea, but I'll keep that to myself at this point until I have more proof of my suspicions," Maggie said. The captain nodded his head in agreement, just glad that he had shifted the responsibility of finding the kook who had been causing a crisis in his resort town to the M&J Investigations folks.

"Of course, you'll keep us informed of any progress you're making?" the captain asked.

"Of course," Jonathan said. Maggie and Jonathan left the scene of the boa constrictor fiasco, got back into the Crown Vic, and Maggie roared away back toward their office.

PART II – The Fear of the Unknown

Chapter 11
Exposing the Perp's Identity

Taking the reins of the search for a very emotionally disturbed criminal upon themselves, the M&J Investigations Agency was now in full command of the effort to find and stop the perp from causing more damage to the city of Gulf Shores or its citizens. As with any investigation, one needs to find a starting point to focus on and move forward based upon logical conclusions from the data presented. The problem Maggie and Jonathan had was that this guy was a rogue figure with little or no background of crime to lead them to him based upon his past evil deeds. He appeared to have a vendetta based on some unspoken act done to a friend or family member. Those were difficult people to detect and detain until *after* they had caused a lot of grief for everyone affected. Maggie related this perp to a potential shooter who walks into a school, church, or mall and opens fire with a semi-automatic weapon. The signs were there with most of the major shootings in the world, but those close to the shooters were either oblivious to how unstable they were or didn't really care to know. Logic dictated to Maggie and Jonathan that if they could get one step ahead of the perp in Gulf Shores that they could possibly prevent more unnecessary carnage. The key was discovering just whom they were looking for as the perp.

Maggie, Jonathan, Jo-Ellen, and Maria were all sitting around the coffee table in the reception area of the office the next morning, brainstorming ideas of how to begin to look for a crazed man who wanted to kill his fellowman for no good reason. They had gone through two pots of coffee before Jo-Ellen spoke up.

"In a short sentence, tell us what this perp is probably trying to prove with his outlandish stunts?" Jo-Ellen's question was not out of place after the repetitive incidents the day before in Gulf Shores. An allegator almost decapitated a child in a private swimming pool, two tigers were roaming inside the discount mall found just south of Foley. No reports of injuries, and the local police force in Foley captured the beasts by baiting large animal cages with raw steak. The policeman who saw the event said the animals ate like they were starving. There were as many as ten different reports on wild animals roaming the cities of Foley and Gulf Shores throughout the day. By nightfall, all the unaccounted animals had been found, recaptured, and sent packing to the Mobile Zoo. The owner of the private petting zoo could not be found for an explanation or to give the inquiring police officers any description of the possible perp who "borrowed" them for his little prank. As one of the police officers in Gulf Shores said, "It could have been much worse. Someone may have gotten injured, or we may have had to kill an animal in public in front of everyday citizens. Everyone believed that the best possible outcome that could have happened did occur. That didn't negate the fact that someone was going around making a mockery of the police departments of proud South Alabama cities, putting those in command of the facilities in very awkward positions. Now, the brain trust for M&J Investigations was trying to piece enough facts together to come up with a decent lead.

"That's the problem, Jo-Ellen," Jonathan said. "The actions of the perp make no logical sense. Why would he threaten to kill innocent people with arsenic, then turn wild animals loose on an unsuspecting and innocent public?" While not a detective herself, Maria spoke up with as good a reason as anyone as to why someone would put a city through this chaos.

"Can we all agree that this guy was trying to capture the attention of everyone in the area with his stunts?" Maria asked. They all nodded yes. "Then, why not play to his weakness. Tempt him by agreeing to help him get his wishes fulfilled if he would refrain from harming innocent people."

"How are we going to get a message to him without knowing who he is?"

"How did he get his first message to us?" Maggie asked.

"If I remember correctly, he put a note on Jonathan's car windshield," Jo-Ellen said. "We have no idea if he even owns a car or truck."

"I think Maria has a good idea, but we're missing the point on how to contact him," Maggie said.

"Are you suggesting that we run an ad in the local newspaper and make our offer to him?" Jonathan asked.

"Kind of sort of," Maggie replied.

"What does that even mean?" Jo-Ellen laughed heartily at her mentor's statement.

"Why do we think he's doing all of these things?" Maggie asked.

"To get attention or to try and convince someone to respect his threats," Jo-Ellen said.

"Exactly. So, if he thinks the city might respond to him, he would be reading the newspaper from cover to cover to detect a positive response from those whom he is trying to persuade to come around to his thinking. We run a small, four-line advertisement, saying that we will be willing to listen to his complaints against the city of Gulf Shores. Hopefully, we will detect who the perp is while he is communicating with us, we can swoop in, and we can put him in cuffs!" Maggie smiled, thinking her idea was fantastic.

"While I see some flaws in the overall plan, I think it's as good a plan as I've heard so far to go about identifying and capturing this perp," Jonathan said. "Who writes the four-line ad?" They all looked at Jo-Ellen, and she nodded her approval.

"Why don't I construct a couple of ads and we can choose which one we all think will bring the perp out into the open."

"I like that idea," Maggie said. "Get going. We need to make the afternoon deadline for the local newspaper."

The *Islander* had been established in 1977, and it principally served Gulf Shores, Orange Beach, and Ft. Morgan. There were street boxes where one could buy the paper in Foley and Fairhope, but most of the circulation was focused in the three largest areas of the immediate Gulf Coast area around Gulf Shores. While the number of copies of the newspaper actually delivered to residences and places of business was not staggering, the *Islander* had a good online presence as well. The demographics of the Gulf Coast area, from Orange Beach, Alabama, through Gulf Shores, to Ft. Morgan was almost totally Caucasian. There were less than three percent of all residents who were Asian, Latino, or African American in heritage. Of course, that's not surprising for a resort city where folks move to retire to get tan and sit in the sunshine, but if one saw a minority walking along the beaches in Gulf Shores or Orange Beach, it was a great probability that the beach walker was a tourist.

"How does this sound for our ad?" Jo-Ellen asked her bosses and partner.

"*If you want someone to listen to your complaints, please contact M&J Investigations in Gulf Shores.*

We are willing to negotiate with you to help you get satisfaction from whatever your issue is with the city and its employees."

Maggie had a frown on her face and Jonathan was contemplating the impact such a statement might have on their suspect. Jo-Ellen could see from their expressions that she needed to tune up her advertisement.

"How about something like this:"

"Don't be afraid to come forward and speak to the M&J Investigation Agency if you are upset with the political happening in the city of Gulf Shores. We will act in your behalf to help you solve your problems."

"Too subtle. We need to get this perp's attention and have him make a commitment to talk to us sooner than later," Maggie said. "Try again." Jo-Ellen was getting frustrated trying to read Maggie and Jonathan's minds on how to approach the perp when she had a brilliant idea. She'll just ask him to come forward, state his case, and work out the details with the city manager for Gulf Shores.

"Why don't we just tell him that we know he's upset with something the city did to him or one of his friends, and we are willing to negotiate with the city for him, but that he will have to come forward and explain what he's trying to accomplish with all the violence." Maggie, Jonathan, and Maria looked at Jo-Ellen as if she had to heads. However, before JoEllen started to defend herself, Maggie began to smile and nod her head.

“It might just work after all,” she said. “Let’s work out some possible logistics and ‘what ifs,’ and then let’s explain it to Jonathan and Maria and see if they think it will work.” All of a sudden, what moments ago seemed frivolous now was a practical attempt to bring the mysterious perp out of the shadows. It was just bizarre enough of an idea to work. Maggie and Jo-Ellen began to fine tune the ad until it read:

“This message is for the distraught person who really believes that he has a legitimate complaint with the city of Gulf Shores. If you will contact us, anonymously, we will try to help you get your message across to the people whom you want to communicate with.”

Jo-Ellen listed the contact information in the ad for M&J Investigations, and they got the ad to the Islander in time to be included in the afternoon publication and distribution of the local paper. The information was also posted almost at once online, so now all they had to do was wait for the perp to contact them.

The advertisement was sent to the *Islander* at 3:00 PM, the posting on their website was done within thirty minutes of the delivery of the advertisement, and their response was almost immediate from the perp.

“You can’t help, because you are part of the problem. Nice try, though.”

"What does that mean?" Jonathan asked Maggie. "How can we be part of a local problem since we haven't been local except when this building was being constructed and when we moved into it as our residence and home office?"

"There has to be a connection between us and the perp. I don't know how or where, but it has to be there," Maggie said.

"The only connection we have with Gulf Shores prior to moving into this condominium was the financial agreement I made with the guy who was going broke trying to complete the units. Do you think that maybe he is the person who the perp is after, and not necessarily the folks associated with the city of Gulf Shores?" Maggie thought for a moment and shook her head no.

"I think there has to be more of a direct link between M&J Investigations and the perp. If we can discover that fact, we'll be on our way to answering all the other questions surrounding the drama the perp is causing in Gulf Shores and the surrounding communities."

"I have a suggestion," Maria said. "If you don't mind a non-detective's input."

"You're as much of this team as anyone else," Jo-Ellen reassured Maria.

"Absolutely," Jonathan said. "What's your suggestion?"

"I imagine the city of Gulf Shores keeps records of construction permits, filings for easements, and other documents related to new construction on file somewhere in city hall, or at least digitally on their computers."

"I'm sure that you're correct, Maria. What did you have in mind?"

"M&J Investigations has an excellent working relationship with the city of Gulf Shores, wouldn't you agree?"

"I would hope so after we have assisted them in many cases these past few years without any financial charge to the city," Jonathan said. "Do we need to call in a favor or two to get this investigation rolling?"

"I was thinking if I could get access to all the building permit requests from before you and Maggie invested in this condominium, we might figure out if there was someone really upset by all of the things that happened before you got involved with the developer of Crown Victoria Condominiums. There are no guarantees that we will find a smoking gun, but it's one thing we can explore. Right now, we have zero leads, right?"

"What would you be looking for, Maria," Jo-Ellen asked.

"I don't know for sure, but what other logic is there to why this perp thinks we are part of the problem? It has to predate us coming to Gulf Shores to set up a business." Without hesitation, Jonathan picked up the office telephone and called CPT Phillips' office.

"This is Captain Phillip's office. How may I help you?" the police chief's secretary asked.

Jonathan asked her if the captain was taking calls, and she said she'd have to check. She was back quickly, and she said she would connect Jonathan with CPT Phillips. The phone line clicked a couple of times, then the captain picked up and began to speak.

"Is this Jonathan Pembroke?"

"It is, Captain. You know when we agreed to take the lead in the investigation of the perp who is tormenting city hall, I mentioned that we had to do things our way. Do you remember that conversation?"

"I do. Why do you ask?"

"We have an idea of how to narrow down the possible suspect who has been persecuting the city with all these incidents. We know the least he can be charged with is manslaughter, in regard to the deaths of the two tourists who ingested arsenic during the shrimp festival, but he may also be the person behind the release of the animals, even if we can loosely tie him to the events, but it would be as starting place."

"That line of investigating does sound promising. What do you need from my office to get started?" This was the part that Jonathan was reluctant to explain to CPT Phillips. They actually needed to review every transaction which related to the properties on the beach over the past ten years. For that, Maria would need to be embedded in their offices with computer access to most of the city's archived files. Jonathan told the chief what he needed, and he thought that CPT Phillips would react negatively with the implied invasion of the files for every department in the city, but he didn't. "Just exactly what are you looking for?" Jonathan chuckled when he answered.

"That's part or the problem. We have no idea what we're looking for."

"How do you go about finding something you're not sure you're looking for?"

"We're hoping that we will recognize the significance of whatever lead we discover. We have a very unique young woman who will be performing that task for us."

"Do I know her?"

"Probably, but I don't remember if you've met her in person before. Her name is Maria Garcia, and she's our office manager and all-around girl Friday. She's the significant other of our detective Jo-Ellen Broussard, and she has had years of research experience, having worked for the public library in a northern city for most of her adult life. If there's something to find, she'll probably find it."

"I want to find this perp for several reasons, the least of which is that he is driving my entire office and patrol personnel bonkers. They seem to be chasing their shadows, because when they think that they have closed in on someone who could be behind these pranks the prankster just evaporates into thin air. So, you and Maria come set up shop in the office until you've identified the perp. Then we'll all figure out a way to catch him and stop this madness!" The chief was obviously getting frustrated that the pranks on the city of Gulf Shores had got so out of hand that the mayor was calling him every day asking what CPT Phillips had done to find and stop the perp.

"We will find him and try to neutralize the problems he is causing with his constant barrage of attacks on the city of Gulf Shores," Jonathan said as he hung up the telephone. "Well, Maria, it looks like you're in!"

Chapter 12
Details, Details

Maggie, Jonathan, and Jo-Ellen asked Maria what she needed to have the best searching abilities at city hall, and she gave them a couple of requests for hardware and software that could be installed on her laptop computer and taken with her when she went to the police precinct. Of all the jobs or careers Maria Garcia had ever wanted, being a private detective was not one of them. She was into hard facts which could be found by researching a subject thoroughly, compiling a list of known specifics about the subject in question, and writing a detailed and exact report. For most people, such a job would be about as exciting as counting beans in a canning factory. However, Maria had that kind of mind. She was a whiz in math and science, and she was even better at numbers. Jo-Ellen was always trying to get Maria to go to a casino with her and count cards so they could win lots of money. Maria reminded her that most of the casinos are run by the mob, and she didn't want any of her delicate fingers broken in multiple places just because she could count cards better than the average casino visitor. Jo-Ellen always promised Maria that she would be there with her Glock if anyone got out line and threatened them, but Maria was far too timid to do anything even bordering on unethical.

The next day Jonathan and Jo-Ellen went with Maria to the police precinct office. Maria had been in the Rowlette, Illinois, offices of the police department in the past when Jo-Ellen was still working there as the Chief Homicide Detective, but all police offices made Maria uncomfortable. Having worked in a business where no one was allowed to speak above a whisper, and even then, any verbal language was discouraged, Maria didn't enjoy hearing the drunks and angry people being arrested and booked at the station. Fortunately, Maria convinced CPT Phillips that she would be much more efficient in a small office with a monitor connected to the computer history archives. He accommodated her, and she was quickly connected to the database and up and running at full speed. Jonathan had suggested that Maria focus on the Gulf Shores beach areas for two years prior to his and Maggie's move to the city, as well as two years after they had moved into the Crown Victoria Condominiums. If there were a connection between their involvement and the condominiums' development, there was a good chance that Maria could get to the bottom of things. Maria didn't know what she was looking for in her search, other than anything that stood out as unusual or a threat to the completion of the Crown Victoria Condominiums, so she set her search parameters very broad and inclusive. She could narrow the search if she began to get bogged down in bureaucratic details. It took Maria eight hours to detect something out of the ordinary, but she was pretty sure she had hit on something of interest, so she called Jo-Ellen and spoke to her about her findings.

"I think found something," Maria said.

"Let me put you on speaker so Jonathan and Maggie can hear the conversation," Jo-Ellen said. Maria heard the receiver click a couple of times, and then she could hear the background noises of the office.

"This is what I've discovered so far. There had been a couple of businesses with licenses to run on the same site as the Crown Victorian Condominiums over the years before the property was sold to the developer. Actually, the city of Gulf Shores seized the property by condemning the existing building, razing it to the ground, and auctioning off the property on the courthouse steps. The owner of the property had been killed in a fire which had destroyed the historic warehouse which had stood on the beach at Gulf Shores for almost 100 years, so the city believed that they were doing a public service clearing the land for development."

"Did the property owner's family benefit from the city's seizure of the property? Do you think that maybe they have something to do with the things going on now with the terror campaign against the city of Gulf Shores?"

"I have just discovered the fact that the city practically stole the property for the deceased owner's family. I'll look into the newspaper articles and other official documents in the city's archives to see if the surviving family members are mentioned there and what happened to them. It's after 5:00 PM now, and the administrative part of the police department is closing down the office for the day. I can resume my search tomorrow after they open at 9:00 AM."

"That sounds like a good plan, Maria. I'll see you at home tonight," Jo-Ellen said and hung up. She looked at Jonathan and Maggie and smiled as broad a smile as they could ever remember Jo-Ellen having on her face the entire time that they had known her.

"She's a keeper," Maggie said to Jo-Ellen, winking at her to acknowledge how much they appreciated Maria's efforts.

"She would do more if she just knew what we expected of her," Jo-Ellen said.

"She's doing just fine, Jo-Ellen," Jonathan said. "We're so blessed that she decided to move south with you when you took the job with M&J Investigations." Jo-Ellen began to gather her things to stop working for the day, and Jonathan suggested that she wait to come into the office in the morning until Maria had settled into the police department's research files the next day. "What I've found with people like Maria is that just a little extra support can help them gain confidence to really succeed at their missions." Jo-Ellen nodded her agreement, and she boarded the private elevator for home. Jonathan turned to Maggie and asked if she would like to go somewhere special for dinner that evening.

"You don't have to ask me twice to accept an invitation to dinner," Maggie said. "What did you have in mind?"

"I discovered a unique dinner place, but I want to surprise you."

"What do I need to wear?"

"Casual clothes are preferred, so you can go as you're currently dressed. Let' go," he said. He punched the elevator button, waited for the dedicated car to open in their suite, and they boarded it for the ride down to the parking garage.

"Who drives?" Maggie asked.

"I do, but we'll take *Lucy* for this trip." Maggie raised her eyebrows when he said that. Jonathan only rarely took the classic 1966 red Corvette out for a drive. When they got into the sportscar, Jonathan carefully pulled out of the basement parking lot and onto Highway 182 and headed toward downtown Gulf Shores. Highway 59 North intersected with Alabama Highway 180, the highway which dead ends at Fort Morgan. Jonathan had the top down, Maggie had her hair pulled back into a ponytail, and the wind blowing across the peninsula was cool and inviting.

"This is something, Jonathan. You haven't taken me on a surprise date in years."

"Don't you think it's about time I did?"

"I guess. After the craziness dealing with the perp in Gulf Shores, this will be a nice respite," and Maggie reached over and squeezed his hand. They drove and drove, and Maggie thought that they would never get there. "I forgot that it is over twenty miles down this peninsula to the fort. Is the surprise actually at Fort Morgan?"

"You'll just have to wait to discover the surprise," he teased. They were about a mile from the end of the peninsula, and Maggie knew that the only thing at the end of the road was a marina and the historically known Tacky Jack's restaurant. There was a Tacky Jack's in Gulf Shores as well, but it was totally different in its approach to service than the one isolated at Ft. Morgan. Ft. Morgan was less prim and proper, but the food was just as good. Jonathan turned left off Hwy 180, the only way one could turn without driving into the bay, and he pulled up to a wharf. There was a paddle boat tied up at the dock, and Jonathan drove right up to the ramp, onto the wharf, and onto the paddle boat. His little red Corvette fit perfectly into a marked parking spot on the lower deck. The first mate greeted them, officially invited them on the boat, and opened the door of the Vette for Maggie.

"Welcome to a little bit of heaven," he said. He motioned them to the main floor of the paddleboat where a table was set formally, to include a linen tablecloth, linen napkins, silver flatware, and fine crystal. Maggie was totally surprised at the sight, and she sat compliantly in the chair which was pulled out for her by their host. Jonathan was beaming as he watched Maggie's reaction to everything around her.

"Did I surprise you?" Jonathan asked. Maggie leaned over the table and gave Jonathan a big wet kiss on the mouth.

"What do you think?" The waiter came and brought a bottle of champagne, two stemmed glasses, and a container to hold the remaining wine in the bottle. He also brought them some appetizers of shrimp, crab, and oysters, fresh bread, and lots of butter.

"I think you have been planning this event for some time, and you have been very efficient keeping it a secret from me," she said with a smile. "What other secrets have you been keeping from me?"

"Nothing else. I just couldn't remember the last time we did anything really romantic, and this seemed like a romantic thing to do."

"I'm assuming this was an expensive endeavor as well."

"Maggie, I'm a billionaire. Why would expense concern me?"

"I was just curious how much something like this would cost the average Joe," she said.

"That's a moot point, since the average Joe couldn't afford it," he said.

"I didn't know that there was a ferry service at Fort Morgan, other than the public ferry which takes cars and their patrons to Dauphin Island across the bay."

"There isn't," Jonathan said.

"Then explain this," Maggie said, using her arm to make a sweeping gesture of the current vessel they were now on. The paddleboat had left the wharf, and it was moving west across the Bay of Mobile.

"Maggie, one can rent almost anything for the right price. It's simply a rental, doing my bidding."

"And may I ask you what your bidding is tonight?"

"I thought we might paddle over to Dauphine Island, cruise around it a couple of times, and head back to port. All the while, we will be feasting on Chateaubriand, steamed local vegetables, and the best champagne this paddleboat has to offer." Jonathan raised his glass in a toast to his and Maggie's adventure. She met his glass with hers, clinked them together, and they both drank the excellent champagne.

Their dinner lasted for two hours, and by the time the waiter was serving cognac, they were pulling back up at the pier where they had disembarked earlier that evening. Jonathan gave the waiter his black American Express card, signed the exorbitant check, and they were quickly back in the Vette and headed home.

"That was a nice surprise, Jonathan. You're right. We're not spontaneous enough anymore.

We'll have to work on that!" Maggie said, again giving him a big kiss on his mouth. As they rode back to the condominium, Maggie considered her personal situation, and she felt good about it. She had been engaged to a warm and caring man for several years, he put no pressure on her to marry and have kids, and he was always surprising her with trips, gifts, and other special events which made her life special.

Maggie had decided years ago that she would probably never marry and have children, because her work was her real family and she didn't think she had time to burp, clean, and change diapers for two or three years. While no one would describe her as anything but feminine, she wasn't a domesticate woman with the urge to be the "little lady of the house" whom her husband came home to every night, expecting a hot meal and an attentive ear to listing to his day's events. She was more of an action-oriented person, and Jonathan seemed to be okay with the situation which they had carved out for themselves over the years. What made tonight even more special was the fact that Jonathan took *Lucy* from the garage to complete the experience.

Those people who had not known Jonathan before he and Maggie became a couple didn't really *know* the Jonathan of old. One reason Maggie didn't want to have anything to do with Jonathan initially was because he had had a reputation in college as being a womanizer.

Because of the vast wealth of his father's estate, Jonathan was able to fly his dates to New Orleans from Chicago for lunch and fly another woman to dinner in New York the same day, if the urge hit him. He was chauvinistic, pompous, and spoiled. Because of his good looks and piles of money, he could have any girl or woman he wanted. He simply overwhelmed them with things of value, sparing no expense if he really wanted to impress a girl. He once flew a model he had been wanting to date to Paris for lunch, and they flew back on his father's private airplane the same day. They had a specially designed jet with a full bar and bedroom on board, and Jonathan make full use of that airplane on several occasions. He was the catch! However, when he was in his senior year at Loyola University in Chicago studying Criminology, he met Maggie Watson, and he was dazzled by her. The ironic part of their early romantic story was that Maggie had not been impressed with Jonathan Pembroke, and she wouldn't give him the time of day.

Maggie had come from a conservative Roman Catholic family, was reared in the Catholic Church, went to a Catholic high school, and had one goal in mind for her future, and it wasn't being a conquest for Jonathan Pembroke. She had told her grammar school and her high school teachers that she wanted to become a great detective like her long, lost relative Dr. John Watson. While there was no hard evidence that she could generate tying her to the famed detective, she knew in her heart of hearts that she was related to the great man. She wanted to follow in his footsteps, but she wanted to lead, like Sherlock Holmes, not play second-fiddle to someone else who was the great detective. In reality, Maggie knew that the entire Sherlock Holmes mystery web was created by the brilliant mind of Sir Conan Doyle, but she still alluded to her famous relative when asked why she wanted to be a detective.

Maggie had rebuffed Jonathan Pembroke while still in college, and he went on to graduate from Loyola University, entered Harvard and finished a master's degree in Psychology, and received his law degree from the university a few years later. He married the hand-picked society girl arranged by his father and her father, uniting two fortunes and political power, but it wasn't to be. He was miserable, finally got a divorce and he sought out his old college sweetheart, Maggie Watson.

Johnathan was not received well by Lt. Maggie Watson of the Rowlette Police Department when he first offered his services pro bono to help with a complicated murder case, but she finally relented and let him be a part of the investigation. One thing led to another, and they finally became close friends and colleagues. It took several years before Jonathan could convince Maggie that he had changed and was no longer a self-centered jerk. After working together at the city of

Rowlette, Illinois, for several years, they began to date and developed a close personal relationship. After twenty years of service with the city of Rowlette, Maggie and Jonathan decided to retire to Gulf Shores, Alabama, and take things a little slower. That's how M&J Investigations came about. As far as anyone could tell, Maggie and Jonathan had a wonderful relationship going, but there was still no marriage or kids mentioned in their futures. That was a lot to remember and consider, but those were the thoughts going through her mind as they motored back toward the condominium at Gulf Shores.

"Jonathan, why didn't you get turned off by my rudeness when you first approached me in Rowlette? I was doing my best to rebuff you and drive you away."

"That's a long time ago, Maggie. Why do you ask?"

"I would never have predicted that we would be driving in a red Corvette convertible in South Alabama ten years ago when you first approached me when I was the Chief Homicide Detective in Rowlette. See how wrong people can be when they judge others?" she said, patting him on the thigh as he drove.

"You really weren't wrong, Maggie. I was a rich, spoiled kid and I needed to have a dose of reality served to me. You just happened to be the perfect server!" He smiled at her warmly and continued. "I will admit that when I first saw you in Rowlette, I didn't know what I wanted from you. What I did know is that I didn't want what my father had planned for my life—power politics and social ladder-climbing. I guess meeting and spending time with Senators, Presidents, and corporate bigshots was entertaining, but after a while it just gets old. The wife chosen for me by my father was beautiful, politically connected, and from a wealthy family. There was just no love there, and material things can only satisfy so much. I wanted the real thing. I wanted you. I had wanted you from the first day I met you, even though I would have messed things up royally had I succeeded in convincing you to date me at that time. The best thing you did for me was to shut me down. It took a few more years for me to learn the important things of life are not money and things, but the personal relationship one builds with another like mind."

"I'm glad it worked out Jonathan. I am very happy and content with our relationship. Do you still have no regrets about not being officially married and us not having kids?"

"The way I see that situation, Maggie, is that it would simply be gravy for our relationship. The best thing I ever did was place my wealth into a trust and try to live a normal life." She laughed.

"Well, living in a 20,000 square foot condominium, driving a vintage, priceless Corvette, and providing the financial means for small cities and police precincts to go after criminals they otherwise wouldn't have the capacity to do is hardly what I would refer to as a *normal* life."

"Maybe but being able to give back to society and share all of that with you is normal to me, and I wouldn't change anything about it." She gave him another kiss on the cheek, and they suddenly had arrived at home.

Jonathan and Maggie caught the elevator to their floor, and they decided it would be good to take Molly on a short walk down the beach. She had been cooped up in the condominium for hours and she needed a little "people time" with her favorite couple. They walked past the Hangout, down the beach sidewalk until it ended at a high-rise condominium, then they turned north and walked to Highway 182. The traffic was almost non-existent at 11:00 PM, and as they walked, they noticed the breeze coming in from the Gulf of Mexico was a little cooler than normal. The summer was coming to a close, and the storms in the Gulf were beginning to form and move inland. Hurricane season was still active until November, and they hoped what they were feeling was not a sign of things to come.

Chapter 13
Digging Deeper

Maggie and Jonathan heard rustling going on in the office at 8:00 AM,
so, Jonathan slipped on his robe and bedroom slippers and walked into the kitchen. He was surprised to see Maria working feverishly on her desktop computer, merging files and combining data that she obviously had discovered the day before at city hall.

"Aren't you an early bird," he said. "What gets you going so early this morning?"

"I need to be in city hall by 9:00 AM, but I wanted to summarize what happened yesterday before I forgot anything. I think I may be getting to some important information about the city and its policies of condemning property, selling it at auction, and profiting handsomely from the difference of the true value of the property and what they pay the previous owners for it. It's all legal and nothing violated the laws themselves, but the spirit of the law seems to be taking a beating on most of these condemned properties. I'll know more later today," she said, standing up and grabbing her briefcase and heading for the elevator. "Wish me luck!" Then she was gone. Jonathan rubbed his eyes, debated whether or not to have a cup of coffee, and then slipped quietly back into the bedroom and got into bed with Maggie.

“What was that all about?” she asked sleepily.

“I never knew our quiet little office manager could get so fired up over an assignment. We should speak to Jo-Ellen about including Maria in more of our operations. She is having a blast going after the archives in the city’s files, and she said she may have found something interesting to share with us. She said she would know by the end of the day.”

“Was Jo-Ellen with her?”

“Nope. Just Maria transposing her notes from yesterday’s time spent at city hall yesterday. She’ll put a report together for us, and we should have a better idea of what we’re dealing with at that time. I was just amazed how she took to the research part of this investigation. She’s a natural.”

“Speaking of a natural,” Maggie said, “I think it’s time you and I got up and started our day as well.”

“In the shower?” Maggie rolled her eyes and pulled the cover back over her head.

Jo-Ellen came into the office as Maria was leaving to return to city hall. Maria gave her a quick summary of the things she had discovered the day before, and she told Jo-Ellen that she hoped to put everything in perspective by the end of the day. The two young women exchanged a hug, Maria headed downstairs to her car, and Jo-Ellen got off the elevator at M&J’s office. With

Maria doing the upfront work with the city of Gulf Shores by analyzing their historical construction files, there wasn't much for Jo-Ellen to do at the present time. She poured herself a cup of coffee, walked out on the private patio, and took a comfortable chair looking west into the waters of the Gulf of Mexico. She could hear the waves slapping the sand beaches in an unending cacophony of musical sounds, and for a moment she was being hypnotized by the repetitiveness of the sound of the tide coming in. She was jostled back into reality when Maggie took the chair beside her and said good morning.

"And good morning to you as well," Jo-Ellen returned the greeting. Soon Jonathan joined them, and they basically watched the seagull's flit about with their squawking and yakking as they dove for fish or begged to be fed by unassuming tourists.

"You have to admit that seagulls are more like us than we want to believe," Jonathan said.

"How's that?" Jo-Ellen asked

"They not only want to eat, but they also want to be recognized and worshipped!"

"I don't know if I agree with your interpretation of their language, but they do make a racket, and it gets obnoxious after a while," Maggie said. "Do you think the perp finally got tired of the city of Gulf Shores making a racket and being obnoxious, and that's why he's chosen now to attacked them?"

"There has to be some reason for the perp to just now decide to go commando on the city for something that happened several years ago. Why wait three or four years to act on your disgust and hatred? I think we're missing something here. Maybe Maria will get us a starting point for our investigation. I was very impressed with her this morning as she was preparing to get back to things at city hall. I was telling Maggie that we should get Maria more involved in some of our cases in the future. What do you think, Jo-Ellen?"

Jo-Ellen was very protective of her significant other, and she never wanted to put Maria is a tough spot where she might be embarrassed or humiliated by failing in a task asked of her by Jonathan or Maggie. Jo-Ellen had never thought of Maria as being anything but a secretarial or research type person, so the thought of her actively working a case alongside Maggie and Jonathan was hard for her to imagine.

"That would strictly be up to Maria, should she have an interest in taking part in an active case. If I remember correctly, she volunteered to get involved with this case because she felt comfortable doing the background research needed to come up with a starting point for our investigation to begin. I think what we might want to do is let her know that she is welcomed to volunteer to get involved in any case we are pursuing, and then if she decides to join in with us, all the better." That seemed logical and acceptable to Jonathan and Maggie.

"I think either Maggie or I should speak to her and let her know what we just discussed. Then, if she's inclined to jump into a case, she'll know that she's always welcome to do so. Do that work for you?" Jo-Ellen nodded her acceptance of that suggestion, and she told Maggie that she would speak to Maria at home about their decision to include her more, and then Jonathan or Maggie could reinforce it at the office. This seemed like a good solution to everyone. What was nice was the unexpected added help in detective work that Maria could do with little or no specialized training. She had been around that kind of work most of her adult life, having been with Jo-Ellen for years, so things of an investigative nature just came naturally to her. They all continue to rock in their chairs as they saw the sun rising over the Gulf and they noticed the heat of the day beginning to make its presence known.

* * *

Maria arrived at city hall right at 9:00 AM, said hello to everyone whom she had met the day before, and she headed back to the makeshift office CPT Phillips had created for her to do her research. Maria had never been a talkative person or someone who was comfortable leading a conversation in a group, so she just kept her head down and did her work. She found many letters of complaints sent to the city in regard to the massive revitalization of the Gulf Shores public beach areas, but there was one complainant who stood out amongst the other ones in the archives. His name was Leon Douglas, a trainer and owner of a gym operating in a previously abandoned warehouse just to the north of the Pink Pony Pub, on the very spot where the Crown Victoria Condominiums now stood. It was obvious to Maria that this was no coincidence. Maria cross-referenced the Islander newspaper articles in and around the time of the dispute Douglas was having with the city of Gulf Shores, and she discovered that Leon Douglas had been tragically killed in a fire in that very building, his operating gym, the night of the fire which destroyed the old building. Maria looked for the cause of the fire, and then she read where the building had very old and dangerous electrical wiring, so no foul play was assumed to have taken place, and therefore no case of arson to be investigated. The city condemned the lot and remains of the building where the gym had once been, offered the surviving family a pittance for the land, officially seized it as a safety concern and it became the property of the city of Gulf Shores. As Maria continued to dig into the history of the property where the Crown Victoria Condominiums were built, she was able to follow a series of events where the land was offered for sale on the steps of the Baldwin County Courthouse in Bay Minette, which is the county seat, the land was purchased by a development company, and the city was paid multiple times the amount of money that they had offered the survivors of Leon Douglas when they had foreclosed on the property. There was no mention of any reconciliation of funds between the city and the family of Douglas, so the city just appeared to have taken the profits from the sale of the condemned property and added it to the city's coffers. While such activities by government authorities didn't surprise Maria, it was a blatant theft of assets from an already devasted family. They had lost the husband and father of the family to a tragedy, and the city of Gulf Shores had added insult to injury by stealing from them in broad daylight. Of all the motives for murder, revenge and financial gain are two of the most often discovered as the reasons for such actions. Had Maria discovered something important back at the beginning of the Crown Victoria Condominium's construction period, or was all this just circumstantial? She would keep digging until she knew for sure.

Maria wanted to make sure she preserved anything she had found suspicious in her research so far, and she called Jo-Ellen and asked if Jonathan and Maggie could join Jo-Ellen and herself for lunch to discuss her findings so far. Jo-Ellen set things up, and she came by city hall and picked Maria up at noon to meet the others for lunch. They chose to eat at the Pink Pony Pub, sit out on the deck, and eat while listening to the Gulf of Mexico sounds of waves crashing and seagulls screaming as they dove into the water to find their meals for the day. When Jo-Ellen and Maria arrived at the pub, Jonathan and Maggie were already sitting under an umbrella in an attempt to block out some of the sun's dominant rays. They were eating from a plate of boiled shrimp and sipping on tall glasses of iced tea.

"Hey, you two," Jonathan said in welcome. "We decided to get an early start on the shrimp, just in case they ran out before you two got here," he said with a smile. Everyone knew that tons and tons of live shrimp were caught in nets just off the coast every day, so the odds of shrimp becoming scarce in Gulf Shores was zero.

"What shall we order. Maria and I are famished," Jo-Ellen said.

"I was thinking some appetizers, a couple of fried fish platters, and some hushpuppies and French fries to complement them. How does that sound?"

"Great!" said Maria.

"Good, because I've already ordered the food and it should be out here pronto," Jonathan said. He was never one to wait when it came to ordering food for his lunch and dinner guests. They had all just gotten comfortable around the table when the food arrived. "What'll you ladies have to drink?"

"Just water for me," Maria said. Jo-Ellen ordered water and tea. They all began to add friend shrimp, fried grouper, scallops, oysters, and crab claws to their plates while they waited for Jo-Ellen's and Maria's drinks to be brought to the table.

"What's this I hear about you having discovered something interesting about the origins of the Crown Victoria Condominiums?" Jonathan asked. Maria had just taken a big bite of food into her mouth so she had to chew and swallow before she could answer his question. Once she could speak again, Maria explained what she had discovered so far.

"Right now, it's just a theory, but I think it's a pretty good one. The facts are these. The city of Gulf Shores forced the surviving family members of a property owner who had been killed in a warehouse fire to sell their property on the beach for a fraction of what the property was worth. The property had been damaged by the same fire which took the owner's life, and the city condemned the land and bought it for future development for the city of Gulf Shores. That piece of land is the exact property where the Crown Victoria Condominiums stand today."

"And you really think the perp who has been terrorizing the city of Gulf Shores may have somehow been connected to the condemning and rezoning of that property? Why hadn't I heard about this before?"

"That I cannot say, but I will say that there are multiple records of demonstrations and acts of foul play going on while the condos were under construction. According to the *Islander* archives, small groups of locals were constantly picketing and harassing the construction crews for the first few months of their work on the building. What do you remember about the situation when you got involved and helped them finance the development?"

"Not that much. What happened was that Maggie and I had decided to move to the Gulf Coast, and we wanted to find the right place for both an office and residence, and we wanted to be on the water. Unfortunately, unless one gets in when a project is being planned and developed, most of the structural things that have to happen to create the perfect office/home situation are already finished before you look at it to change it for your own personal purposes. We needed a professional office location, proper security, a specialized area for Molly, and we wanted all of that to be close enough to the water so we could see and hear the surf from our balcony."

"Did you move directly into the condominium unit when you made your final move to Gulf Shores?"

"Oh, no," Maggie said. "We stayed in a rental unit down the beach from the Hangout and the public beach areas of Gulf Shores while the Crown Victoria Condominiums were being built. As I recall, the construction project had run out of money and was sitting idle when Jonathan first had the idea of investing in its development and creating a fabulous living and working area for us on the 18th floor."

"So, you just went up to the builder and suggested that he make those changes for you?" Maria asked. Jonathan chuckled before he answered.

"That's not how businesses work most of the time, Maria. What I did was offer to finance the completion of the building for a percentage of ownership, with the caveat that they let me do whatever I wanted to do with the top floor. I sat down with Maggie, and we talked about things, and then I didn't mention the condo to her again until it was totally completed, furnished, and ready for us to move in. It blew her away!" Maggie nodded and smiled at Jonathan's comments as she gobbled down a juicy boiled shrimp smothered in cocktail sauce.

"He took me by, and I thought we were going to plan how and where to move furniture into the unit, but when the elevator stopped on the 18th floor and the door opened into the foyer of our personal space, I was flabbergasted. Needless to say, I told him it was perfect, because it was!"

"And no time during the construction of the high-rise did you see or hear of any controversy about the building site?" Maria asked.

"Not a word," Jonathan said. "It probably wouldn't have kept me from going forward with our plans because the site location and the building were exactly what we wanted in a home and office. However, had I known that there might have been some malfeasance on the part of the city of Gulf Shores, I might have looked into any such claims. I had our lawyers check everything out, there were no building leans against the property, and the main reason they had not been able to finish the project was that they were undercapitalized. A few million dollars later, everything was moving forward as smooth as a mountain lake on a quiet summer morning. It took nine months before we could begin to lease individual properties in the building, but within a year all the units were sold, occupied, and everyone seemed to be happy with the outcome of the project. Our real estate corporation actually manages this building, along with several other ones I have invested in after we moved south from Rowlette, Illinois. It sounds like your research may reveal that the city of Gulf Shores owes some reparations to the heirs of the property which was foreclosed on before the Crown Victoria Condominiums were ever planned. Please continue to look into that for me, and that may also help us smoke out the perp." Maria assured Jonathan that she would follow through on the origin of the property where their condo was built, and they continued to eat and enjoy the wonderful fresh seafood while they talked about Maria's discoveries.

"What I would be interested in knowing is if there are any specific local names of individuals who were involved in the aggressive nature of the protests at the time of construction of the condos," Jo-Ellen said. "If you recall what the newspaper advertisement answer was when we tried to contact the perp to work out some compromise, he said M&J Investigations was part of the problem. That tells me that he was probably around during the picketing and demonstrations against the completion of the condo," Jo-Ellen said.

"Where does that leave us with finding the perp? Does that information help us or harm our investigation?" Jonathan asked.

"I think it narrows our search somewhat, assuming the person who is still upset about the acquisition of the property and the construction of the building was probably involved from the beginning of the protests. If we can figure out if he is an heir, or a distant relative of the original owner, that might help us figure out his identity," Maggie said.

"For some reason, I don't get the impression that our perp is a direct family heir or member," Maria said.

"Why?" Jo-Ellen asked.

"Logic, for one thing."

"Please elaborate, Maria. I'm not doubting that you may be on the right track, but where did you get your facts to draw such a possibility."

"I just put myself in the place of the family members who were robbed of their estate by the city's condemnation of their property and later sale of the property to a development company. According to the archives, all of that went on several years ago. Why would the family of someone so mistreated by the city of Gulf Shores wait four or five years to begin to put up a fuss about what happened that many years ago. If they had been that upset at the time, why not take some action before now? No, something is not right about the reaction this late after the time the condominiums were under construction, the units were finished and sold, and the two or three years since all of that happened. What are we missing here? You three are the detectives. I'm just a clerk!" Maria laughed when she minimized her duties at M&J Investigations.

"You are officially our office manager, and a damn good one, too," Jonathan said. Everyone agreed and expressed their agreement vocally.

"Maria is correct about one thing, and that is that we should be looking at what's not here, rather than just the clues we have gained from the perp's actions so far. He's controlling the narrative, and we can't let that continue," Maggie said.

"How do we go about that chore?" Jo-Ellen asked.

"I think Maria is in the best position to help us find a clue or foothold so we can build from there," Jonathan said. "I think it's time to let her get back to city hall and her research project. Anyway, all the fresh seafood has been consumed, and unless I order more food, the Pink Pony Pub will want us to surrender this table for more hungry guests." Everyone agreed, they all rose from their chairs, and Jonathan left enough cash on the table for the food and a nice tip. Jonathan and Maggie headed back to the office, and Jo-Ellen took Maria back to city hall.

"You're doing good work, Maria," Jo-Ellen said, patting her on the shoulder. "Go get 'em, girl!" Maria waved to her significant other as she headed back inside the building.

Chapter 14
Time for Another Dose

Patience was not Arthur Murry's greatest talent, if he had any at all. In all reality, when one makes a serious threat, it usually takes a while for people to decipher if the threat is real or fake, and then they have to work out how, if any, way they intend to address the specific threat. In the case of the two earlier threats Arthur had made before to the city of Gulf Shores, he made the threat, and almost immediately carried out his pledge to act if his threat wasn't taken seriously. The newest threat he intended to make would go much farther to convince the city officials that he meant business. Lives would be lost if they didn't respond in the correct way, and if they didn't do it promptly.

Arthur had become paranoid, and he was beginning to believe that the authorities were closing in on him. He believed that he had to act promptly, or his entire mission to honor and perpetuate the good work Leon Douglas had accomplished would be jeopardized. He had been visiting the public library in Gulf Shores researching how to make effective explosives, where to place them in buildings and other structures for the most effective damage that could be caused by such an act of violence. The logical place for such an attack would be the Crown Victoria Condominiums, but he wasn't sure how good their security was. After walking the Crown Victoria Condominiums property on several occasions, he noticed CCTV cameras everywhere, and, assuming they were real cameras and were being monitored 24/7, he might be noticed or even identified before he could plant his homemade bomb. So, he knew what he wanted to do for his next act of violence against the people in Gulf Shores, but he wasn't sure where he could pull off the event without being detected planting his device or being detected leaving the scene of the event before the explosion happened. He had bought most of the necessary items for his homemade bomb at the local hardware store and other items which could be picked up easily at a local grocery store, but he wasn't convinced he was ready to begin building his device. He had more study to do before he could move forward with his plans.

Arthur couldn't understand how stupid the government was when it came to figuring out how to stop folks from building homemade bombs and other explosive devices. Anyone with a fifth-grade education could go on the Internet and download specific instructions of how to build everything from pipe bombs to Molotov cocktails, and even fertilizer bombs. Arthur guessed that the opportunity to create evil devices was the price the freedom to act on one's thoughts and dreams on the Internet was just part of the formula for individual freedoms most American's enjoyed. He was pleasantly surprised how easy it was to create something so destructive from ordinary soap, diesel fuel, lighter fluid, ball bearings, and fertilizer. Clorox and other household chemicals were also useful when designing bombs and poison gas devices.

Arthur also knew that most perps were detected after the effects of an explosion by the authorities tracing their search history from their laptop or home desk computers. Every computer had a specific IP address, identifying the device, where the data was transmitted to and from, and with those types of facts, the authorities could track almost everything a person did online. So, that's why Arthur used the public library computers for his Internet research. He understood the IP address was an identifier which allowed a website to send data to a specific device, but he calculated that many people used the computers at the public library. What were the odds anyone would even think to track the library IP addresses, and he figured he could get lost in the maze of the number of different people using the computers? Arthur was correct in one assumption, the large number of patrons using the same computer could make finding and naming an individual who searched for explosive devices complicated and almost impossible. Fingerprints on the keys wouldn't help, because there were probably partial fingerprints for hundreds of hands that had touched the keys as they searched the Internet. For now, he was content that his identity was safe in regard to the public library computer searches.

This brought Arthur to another crossroads in his planned revenge against the city of Gulf Shores. Did he want to continue to get their attention, hoping that soon they would surrender the property or value which they had received from it, for all of those beach lots the city had condemned to make way for the new high-rises and other commercial building? Or was it time to actually make the city pay for its sins. Maybe bring down a commercial building, like the one in Oklahoma City a few years ago. That was done with a homemade bomb. It's true the federal building bomb was much larger than what Arthur felt comfortable building, but his bomb would be large enough for his demonstrable exhibit. Killing one or a dozen folks made no difference, as long as the authorities made things right quickly. He was sorry things had come to this juncture, but it was the city's fault. He had been warning them for weeks that there would be consequences if his warnings were not heeded.

Based on his understanding of the concussion possibilities of his homemade bomb, it might be strong enough to take down a bridge, if placed in a strategic area where the load-bearing weight of the bridge was centered, or it could take down a high-rise apartment or condominium building with the proper placement of the charge. There were small bridges all over the Gulf Shores and Orange Beach area, but the most impressive bridge was the one which crossed the Intercoastal Waterway which divided the city of Gulf Shores with the other retail and shopping areas of Gulf Shores and the city of Foley. He could not only probably kill a few people when the bridge came down unexpectedly, but Highway 59 would be made impassable for months to come, and the tourist travel to the beaches could be impaired for many months. The economic impact of such an act was unimaginable, but it was possible. There would be many people who could lose their jobs because the restaurants, hotels, and other tourist attractions might be impossible to visit if the bridge over the Intercoastal Waterway became impassible for any lengthy period of time. He wasn't sure he would choose the bridge for his target, but it was a definite possibility.

Except for its exceptional security systems, the Crown Victoria Condominiums would be ideal large building to attack for his purposes. After all, the land which was deeded to the development company which lay under the foundation of the Crown Victoria building was sacred land—Leon Douglas's inheritance which had been stolen right from under the noses of his surviving family members. Arthur had already tried to check out that building, but the CCTV cameras seemed to be everywhere, and they ran 24/7. However, there were other high-rise buildings available as targets, and most of them had little or no security at all.

He'd probably injure or kill more in an apartment building or condo, but opportunity would play a big role in the target he chose. Arthur believed that he and the city of Gulf Shores had entered into another level of war since they had ignored his earlier pleas to negotiate a fair settlement for those poor families that had been systematically robbed by the government. Arthur wasn't without feelings, and he decided that he would give the city of Gulf Shores one more dynamic warning before he took his next murderous step.

* * *

The Gulf Shores Shrimp Festival was coming to a close and no other visitors to the beach had gotten terribly sick or died from poisoning since the first day of activities. The mayor congratulated the police chief and his department for keeping the city and its visitors safe from more damage from the crazed person who appeared to be holding a grudge against the city of Gulf Shores. While CPT Phillips was happy that the mayor appeared to be happy with the outcome of the week's activity at the beach, the captain wanted to say to the mayor that he and his people had done nothing specifically to deter any more crime. The perp seemed to have simply moved on and things were appearing to be returning to normal at the public beaches. And then it happened.

Flying over the beach, pulling long signed which could be read from the ground, the advertising airplanes were simply a fixture of visiting the beach. In anyone given thirty-minute period of time on most sunny days, four or five small airplanes would pull the banners behind their crafts up and down the beach for what seemed like an eternity. There were no ordinances preventing such advertisement, so the noise and disturbances were accepted as part of one's beach experience. However, this particular day something had changed. The small plane was dropping some form of leaflets from his airplane, and it appeared that there were thousands of them. The pilot appeared to begin dropping the leaflets near the end of the strand where Ft. Morgan was located, and then he continued all the way to Orange Beach, repeatedly dumping thousands of these small pieces of paper from his plane. By the time most of the pieces of paper had landed and had been read by those capturing them on the ground, the small plane had disappeared and had landed somewhere nearby.

Jonathan and Maggie had gone back to their home office, put Molly their beloved Westie on a leash, and were walking her down the beach when the flyers began to fall all around them. Molly began to chase them and bark at them, so Maggie picked one up and was horrified to see the message which had been delivered to thousands of people near the beach properties.

This is a fair warning to everyone who reads this message. The authorities in Gulf Shores have repeatedly stolen property for their own financial gain to sell to developers, pocketed the money, and caused pain and suffering to many through their past actions. They have been given the opportunity to correct their wrongs, but they refuse to acknowledge or admit to any wrongdoing. Therefore, they must be punished, and you will be caught up in the punishment if you choose to remain in the Gulf Shores/Orange Beach area. This will be your only warning.

There was no signature on the flyer, no one claiming the earlier acts of violence against the city of Gulf Shores was connected to the note, but Jonathan and Maggie had been detectives long enough to sense that this was possibly the last desperate act of a deranged person who might injure or kill countless numbers of innocent civilians just to prove a point to the city of Gulf Shores. This maniac had to be discovered and interrupted before he did more damage to their new home city. They didn't know it at the time when they read the note, but Maria had had a breakthrough in her research, and Jo-Ellen had figured out a way to backtrack the killer's movements.

Chapter 15
Deductive Reasoning

When Maria had returned to work after the great feast at lunchtime at the Pink Pony Pub, she began to isolate how someone might use the Internet for evil purposes and yet remain undetected. Having been a professional librarian for most of her adult life, she understood why people often used their public computers to research items that they didn't want a history of pointing to their own IP address on their home computer. Unless the user was quite clever, the users could usually be reduced to just a few persons, and they all had to sign onto the public library intranet to connect to the broader Internet. All it took was a lot of patience and a little bit of luck to isolate those users. Armed with her knowledge of what she was seeing, Maria knew she had discovered how to trace the terrorist if he had used the public library's computers.

There were multiple ways to research a project that individuals had at their disposal if they were just smart enough, and energetic enough, to do it. People no longer remember that almost every word which can be found on the Internet can be found in a real, page-turning, book. It takes much longer, is much more work, and is considered impractical to do research on any serious project without using the Internet in some form or way. Hence, the perp who figured out the arsenic poisoning, and who probably learned about the local privately owned zoo was closing, got most, if not all of his knowledge, from the Internet.

There were ways to disguise oneself when going on the Internet so the IP address of the machine receiving the data was masked, thereby making it more difficult for the computer user to be traced by anyone wishing to see where the user visited, what he downloaded, and what his potential use of that material might be. One of the easier ways to avoid having anyone learn of your Internet search history was to use someone else's computer, like a public library or coffee shop computer. However, many of those who used public computers to surf the Internet didn't realize that just them being in the library or the coffee shop could identify them as a suspect if someone really wanted to know who might have been using a certain machine. When Jo-Ellen and Maria got to the M&J Agency office, Maria was hyped and ready to go even deeper into research on the perp. As they all sat around the fireplace on the comfortable leather couches, Maria shared her idea about the Internet with them. Jonathan and Maggie seemed preoccupied, so Jo-Ellen asked what was on their minds. Maggie had kept one of the flyers, so she handed it to Jo-Ellen, and she showed it to Maria.

"What is that guy trying to do, cause a riot?" Jo-Ellen asked.

“Something like that. Unfortunately, I’m afraid he may actually be willing and capable of carrying out such a threat. We simply must find him and prevent any major damages that he is obviously planning with these new threatened attacks against the city of Gulf Shores,” Maggie lamented.

“Maria thinks she may have narrowed down the search to just a few people, and she has one person who appears repetitively in many of the *Islander* articles speaking out against the sale and potential construction of the Crown Victoria Condominiums. According to the articles she found in the archives, a man named Arthur Murry may be responsible for all these threats against the city of Gulf Shores. After she isolated him from the other potential suspects, we did an Internet search and discovered that he is still in the Baldwin County area. He very well may be our instigator, but we do not have any real imperial evidence placing him at any of the scenes of the crimes. However, my gut tells me that this Arthur Murry is our guy.”

“Why does that name, Arthur Murry, sound so familiar to me?” Jonathan asked no one in particular.

“There is a famous person in history names Arthur Murray, but Murray is spelled differently than the perp we’re trying to find. He was a dancer who made a fortune by opening dance schools to teach the average person in the United States ballroom dancing," Maggie said.

"That is it! I knew I had heard that name before."

"Well, our Arthur Murry is no dancer. He's a domestic terrorist!" Jo-Ellen said. "I just hope I get a chance to shoot him when we corner him." Everyone laughed at her comment, except Jo-Ellen. She was deadly serious.

"So, Maria, you're pretty sure this Arthur Murry is our guy?" Maggie asked.

"As sure as I can be by using circumstantial evidence to and deductive reasoning. I could be wrong, but I'm pretty sure I'm not."

"What are the odds you're right?" Jonathan persisted.

"Somewhere in the 99.5% range," Maria said.

"That's good enough for me," Maggie said. "Now, how do we determine what he was going to do and where he was going to do it." Maggie was only using wishful thinking when she spoke those words, but Maria surprised her with her next comments.

"Maggie, there's a good possibility that we can track the perps Internet activity and we'll get a good idea of what he's planning. As smart as this perp has been so far, I doubt he will use his own personal computer or smart phone to surf the Internet. Unless he has special encrypted files from the Dark net, we should be able to track him." Maggie was astonished.

"How?"

"I need to visit the public library and speak to their resource librarian. She will be able to help us find whoever has been using the Internet lately in the computer section of the library. We can narrow down the search times, compare them to what we know the perp has done with his personal attacks on his associates. From there, we can track the various Internet sites the perp visited from that particular computer's IP address. From that point, you will be getting out of my area of expertise, and you three real detectives will have to try and decide where he is planning his next dramatic display of carnage and evil."

"Do you really think you can do all of that by simply determining where he visited sites on the Internet?" Jonathan asked.

"Absolutely. It's not as difficult as you might think. Every computer has the ability to remember which urls were visited by the use of cookies."

"By urls you mean each separate site the searcher visited?"

"The definition of url is uniform resource locator, and every web address has as separate url assigned to it, much like people have fingerprints. We all have them, but no two sets of fingerprints are identical."

“Okay, I can identify with those definitions,” Maggie said. “How long do you think it will take you to discover how many places our perp visited, and can we determine which pages on each site he viewed?”

“Probably, but I won’t know for sure until I follow in his footprints.” Maggie had heard enough. She told Jo-Ellen to take Maria to the public library and to stay with her until Maria had some hard facts which they could use to go after him legally. Although it was late in the afternoon, Jo-Ellen and Maria left for the library, and that left Jonathan and Maggie time to ponder their thoughts on the balcony overlooking the Gulf of Mexico.

“Do you think we’re chasing rainbows?” Maggie asked Jonathan. She always referred to his logic when she got too invested in an investigation because Jonathan managed to remain optimistic but not so close to the investigation that he couldn’t see the flaws in any approach to solving a problem.

“Actually, if Maria can pull this off, I think her data will be as reliable as any other deductive means of solving the crime. What we really have going for us is the fact that Maria has done this kind of research for years. Granted, it probably wasn’t looking for a killer or terrorist, but the functionality of the searches remains somewhat the same. Let’s just hope she can narrow down the search before this nut does something horrible to more innocent people.”

*   *   *

Maria and Jo-Ellen arrived at the public library around 5:00 PM, and the library was scheduled to close for the day at 6:00 PM. Jo-Ellen showed the head librarian her detective shield, explained that they were researching a very important case, and that time was of the essence. She asked if they could remain after closing hours, assuming Maria couldn't carry out her goal before normal closing time.

"I guess it's OK, especially if there's a possibility that lives may be saved by your staying a little longer." Jo-Ellen thanked her, and then she asked for a list of everyone who had used the public computers in the past forty-eight hours. Jo-Ellen feared that the librarian might find it difficult completing her requests, but to her delight in less than a minute Jo-Ellen had four separate lists of names of users for each computer available to the public. All they had to do now was to do now was match the time of searches on the Internet with Arthur Murry. Every time he had signed into the library's intranet, an electronic record was made of his visits to various sites. Within ten minutes, Maria had learned where Arthur had visited for the past two days, and the places he had chosen to research were scary places for the average Internet surfer.

"Jo-Ellen, look at these sites," Maria said to her partner. "Homemade bomb construction, how to make arsenic from local plants and food stuffs, local animal petting zoos, and other questionable sites. Each one of these urls could be a tie-in to the perp's journey into evil."

"All the more reason to discover his identity and stop him before he can act again. How do we start?" Maria pointed to two library computers sitting side by side on a large table.

"You take the unit to the left, and I'll take the one on the right. There are six personal computers here in the library for personal use by the patrons, so we will just have to operate on the process of elimination. I'm going to write down a code for you to type into a search bar. Once you have typed it, press the enter key and let the computer do its job of searching for any and all sites the IP address has visited. It may take a few minutes, but we should be able to find the correct computer pretty quickly that he used for his Internet research."

"This may seem like a dumb question, but couldn't he have used any or all of these machines at one time or another?"

"It's possible, but it's not probable. If he were a technological genius, he might try to fool us by using various machines to look for specific items on the Internet. After he had found them, he could have combined them in a search which might not raise flags to forensic investigator."

"Are you a forensic investigator?" Jo-Ellen asked. She had been with her partner for years, but they never discussed her library business. Maria figured that it would be boring to a criminal investigator who was constantly chasing bad guys.

"I don't have the legal credentials to call myself a forensic investigator," Maria said. However, I can do everything that they do, and that specialized knowledge makes solving these crimes easier, in most cases." Jo-Ellen was impressed, but not really surprised, that her significant other had the talent to search files forensically. It was a specialized technique which put the odds more in one's favor that just reading files and compiling data. How that data was collected, and how it was interpreted was what made the forensics possible. Chronological searching of facts could sometimes lead a good forensics investigator to probable conclusions that had not even happened up to that point of the search. Nothing was more logical and calculating than a proper computer search with a qualified Internet detective.

"So, it's like you're using deductive reasoning, along with the facts you discover, to calculate a possible outcome?" Jo-Ellen asked.

"Something like that," Maria laughed and handed Jo-Ellen a small piece of notebook paper with a convoluted code written clearly and boldly in her Maria's handwriting. "Let's hook up our computers," which they did. "Now, bring up a search bar." Jo-Ellen went to the Google prompt and opened a search page.

"No, not a Google prompt. A search bar for that specific computer." Maria showed Jo-Ellen how to go to the settings part of the computer's startup menu, type in the special code, and press the enter key. The computer made all kinds of whirring sounds, the monitor flashed on and off multiple times, many separate pages of data were being retrieved, and finally a report was generated for Jo-Ellen to read. She showed it to Jo-Ellen and explained the significance of the report. "This column shows how many times this computer was accessed by the user's specific identifier which the public library assigned to his library access card. This next column shows which urls he visited, what he downloaded, and supplies links to those urls can be revisited by anyone wishing to see where he traveled on the net."

"That's amazing. Looking at the report, so you see anything alarming from the times the perp used that computer?"

"It's hard to say without visiting some or most of the links provided on this list, but I don't see any red flags to be concerned with initially. Let's try the same process with your computer." Jo-Ellen repeated the same process Maria had done with the other computer, and another whirring and flashing of the monitor took place before a list of urls appeared on the screen.

"Should we print out these urls and take them back to the office and visit them to see what the perp was up to?"

"We could, but there's an easier way to discover that information." Maria's hands were flying over the keys, she was typing in various commands, and another list of urls popped up, this one much shorter in length.

"What did you do to change the search?"

"I typed in keywords for the computer to look for the urls it had already found. Words like bomb, explosions, casualties, injuries, and collateral damage generated the list you see on the screen now." There were four links, and Maria clicked on each one and visited the sites. The first one revealed many ways to make homemade pipe bombs, incendiary devices, and fertilizer bombs like the one used in the Oklahoma City Federal Building bombing which claimed 168 lives and injured 680 more innocent civilians, including many children. The next links explained how to create cyanide and arsenic from household chemicals and plants which can be found in the natural landscape or in a common grocery store anywhere in America. The last url link showed all the existing private animal zoos and animal petting parks in the Southern United States, along with the kinds of animals one might find at each location.

"It looks like you hit the motherload," Jo-Ellen said. "And all of these Internet downloads can be officially tied to the library keycard for Arthur Murry?"

"That is correct. In fact, the latest download was just made yesterday, which means the perp probably hasn't had time to gather his material or construct an explosive device yet."

"I'm going to go back to the office and share this information with Jonathan and Maggie. Why don't you see if you can get an idea where Arthur may be planning to strike with his bomb?" Maria agreed and immersed herself again in chasing the urls that Arthur Murry had visited.

Jo-Ellen wasted no time returning to the M&J Agency offices, finding Jonathan and Maggie on the rear balcony overlooking the Gulf of Mexico. They were sipping on some iced drink, probably of an alcoholic nature. After all, it was after dinner and the sun had already set in the West. They asked Jo-Ellen to join them, and she grabbed a wine cooler from the bar before she took a chair facing the beach.

"Do you ever get used to this view?" Jo-Ellen asked as she waved her arm from left to right, taking in most of the beach area and the crashing waves.

"Nope," Jonathan said. "I hope I never get so accustomed to this view that I forget how special it is. By the way, where is Maria? I thought you two went to the public library to do some research."

"We did, and we hit paydirt!"

"Really?" Maggie said. "Don't keep us in suspense, what did you two find?"

"I've got to tell you, even I was surprised by what Maria can do with a computer on the

Internet," she said, further teasing Maggie and Jonathan.

"Stop beating around the bush and tell us already!" Maggie demanded. Jonathan was giggling under his breath. No one ever really got the best of Maggie, but Jo-Ellen was doing a good job teasing her.

"If you must know, Maria was able to get the librarian to give us the code for Arthur Murry's library card, and she figured out a way to find which computer he had used to surf the Internet to research his next planned homemade disaster. It's not good news."

"How much worse can it be than poisoning someone with arsenic or turning beasts loose on an unsuspecting public?" Jonathan asked

"Much worse," Jo-Ellen said, and she got very serious. "He has been researching all types of explosives, to include how to make a pipe bomb, a Molotov cocktail, and a fertilizer bomb like the one that was used in the Oklahoma City Federal Building terrorist act. I remember people talking about it, but I was still in grammar school and didn't understand the impact it had had upon the innocence of our nation. The fact that someone local, an American, could do something like that was far beyond most people's worst nightmares."

"How sure are you and Maria that Arthur is trying to build such a device?" Maggie asked.

"It appeared that he had downloaded several pages of instructions on how to build such a bomb, and he had also searched locally for farm stores that sold high concentrations of nitrogen fertilizer. Under certain conditions, granulated fertilizer can become very unstable and combust very easily. Depending on the amount of ingredients used to make such a bomb, a small explosion can occur or a huge, very destructive one which is capable of taking down a high-rise building or bridge."

"Jonathan, what do you think about having CPT Phillips circulate a picture of profile of Arthur Murry to the landscaping companies, as well as the fertilizer companies, in all of Baldwin County. Perhaps we can get lucky and trace his movements and predict where he might strike depending on what raw material he bought," Maggie said.

"Unfortunately, Maggie, there is no law against buying fertilizer in any quantity, and the other things he may have bought all fall into the same category. In our society, one is innocent until proven guilty, even if all the markers show something odd is happening. We can't arrest a person for thinking about committing a crime. If so, most people would be behind bars at some point in their lives."

"Legally, what can we do?" Maggie asked Jonathan. Jonathan had a law degree and knew the basic "dos and don'ts" when it came to detaining or arresting a suspect. Maggie always took her cue from him when legality became a question.

"If we can find him physically, we can put a tail on him, surveil him like a blanket, and pounce on him if he makes a minor mistake. That's about it."

"What happened to 'If you see something, say something' that we hear about all the time on television? Is that all just a lot of bullshit?" Jonathan couldn't help but laugh at Maggie's overreaction to stopping a crime before it started. Everyone knew if a criminal really wanted to perform a heinous act, it was almost impossible to detect the potential crime and prevent it before it took place. The first amendment was a liability for law enforcement, but assuming someone is going to do something evil and interrupting a potential crime is considered unconstitutional.

"When Maria gets home, we can see if she was able to find what the perp may want to destroy. If he is true to form, he probably searched the Internet for guidance. Maybe we will get lucky," Jo-Ellen said.

"Let's hope we are both lucky and good!" Maggie said.

Chapter 16
Cold Feet

Anyone can get cold feet, or so Arthur thought. Was that happening to him? Where did that idiom come from, anyway? He always understood it as one becoming apprehensive about something, but he didn't know that the saying dated back to the 1600s, and to the writer Stephen Crane in his poem titled "*Maggie: A girl of the Streets*." Of course, it's most common usage came when a potential bride or groom did not show up at the altar to take their marriage vows. Back during the time of the involuntary drafting of young men to go off to war, those who were AWOL were often referred to as *cold-feeters*. No matter the history or what such people were called over the years, Arthur Murry was beginning to wonder if his approach to getting the city's attention was working. He had to consider how to move forward.

Arthur had discovered that Leon Douglas had a nephew by his only sister, and they had lived in Bay Minette all their lives. When Nicholas heard that his uncle had property on the beach in Gulf Shores, Nicholas went to visit him on many occasions. Nicholas was younger than Arthur, and he looked up to Arthur like a brother figure. Once the gym had burned, been condemned, and was sold out from under the heirs of Leon's estate, Nicholas went back home to Bay Minette to live with his mother. Arthur had told Nicholas on many occasions that the city of Gulf Shores should have to pay for what they did to his uncle and his family. While often making empty threats against the officials of Gulf Shores, Nickolas had never known Arthur to actually follow through on any of the threats he had made over the years since the tragedy of his uncle's death. However, Nickolas was now in his mid-twenties, he read the newspapers like everyone else, and he had suspected that the chaos happening in Gulf Shores might have something to do with his uncle's friend.

Nicholas Douglas, he had taken his mother's maiden name as his surname, never really knew his father, and his mother brought him up the best way she knew how as a single mother. She never remarried when her husband left one day for work and never returned home. That was over twenty years ago. Louise Douglas worked in a grocery store as a checker, and she had been there for over twenty years. She was now the head cashier, and, while her income was less than the national average wage, she made enough money to keep a roof over their heads and food on the table. When Nicholas graduated from high school, there was no money to send him off to college, so he got a job at a local tire store to help his mother with their expenses at home. Like many other children who grew up in homes with only one parent, Nicholas was a "latch-key" teenager, left to do his own bidding while his mother was still at work in the afternoons. He was introduced to alcohol, cigarettes, cocaine, and marijuana, all before the age of sixteen. By the time Nicholas left home to move to Gulf Shores he was addicted to many illegal substances, as well as cigarettes and alcohol. He saw nothing wrong with smoking a joint every now and then, and he was not opposed to snorting some cocaine, when he could get it. When Nicholas first visited his uncle Leon, his uncle forbade him to come near his family or his gym if he had been using any kind of drug that day. Leon was an upright citizen of Baldwin County, he was law-abiding, and he didn't think the lifestyle which his young nephew was leading was healthy. Nicholas always honored his uncle's wishes, and he kept himself clean and free of substances his uncle might consider unsuitable for anyone who might be visiting his gym.

Nicholas was a beach bum. You've seen them at street corners with signs up and down the public beach areas, begging for food, money, drugs, or whatever their needs happened to be that day. He had spent several nights in the Gulf Shores and Orange Beach jail cells, and he didn't mind occasionally sleeping safely inside a jail cell and having a hot meal to eat. Nicholas had lost all contact with his mother, and she didn't even know if he were dead or alive, which was fine with him.

One day Nicholas was reading a copy of the *Islander* which had been left on a park bench at the public beach, and a four-line advertisement caught his eye. The ad sounded like someone was threatening the city of Gulf Shores, and the description the advertisement gave for the reasons for the threats reminded Nicholas of the terrible fate of his Uncle Leon. Nicholas had remembered meeting a young man who had idolized his uncle, and he thought the man's name was Arthur something. He couldn't remember his last name, but he did remember that the man raised a commotion when the city condemned his uncle's land and sold it to a developer. If he could only remember his name. For some reason the name Dancer or Prancer kept playing over and over in Nicholas' mind until he remembered Arthur's last name. It was Murry, like the dance studio.

With a lot of time on his hands, Nicholas set out to find Arthur Murry to see if he was the one trying to get compensation for his uncle's gym which had been seized by the city of Gulf Shores. If Arthur was successful, Nicholas, being a relative, should also receive some of the money. Nicholas' thought of instant money and power became a driving force for him to find this Arthur Murry and to help him carry out his task of making the city pay for the damages done to Leon's family. As luck would have it, one day Nicholas saw a man a few years older than himself handing out flyers describing how the city of Gulf Shores had stolen property and money from unsuspecting people over the years. Nicholas went up to the man and spoke to him.

"Tell me about your flyer," Nicholas said.

"It's pretty simple. The city of Gulf Shores is stealing from its citizens and lining its pockets with the profits of the sale of their land and property. It needs to be exposed and stopped!"

"May I ask your name?" Nicholas asked.

"Why do you want to know my name?" the man answered cautiously.

"I'm looking for someone who might have the same philosophy as you. Do you know an Arthur Murry?" The man's eyes brightened, and he smiled.

"I'm Arthur Murry. What do you want with me?"

"My name is Nicholas Douglas, Leon Douglas' nephew. I've been looking for you. Are you the person who place the advertisement in the *Islander* about the city raping the citizens of Gulf Shores in order to steal their property and money?"

"Maybe. What business is that of yours?"

"I *am* an heir to the estate of my deceased uncle, and I thought I'd help you get the city of Gulf Shores to pay up so everyone can benefit from my uncle's efforts to make Gulf Shores more family friendly." While having someone else help him in his quest to achieve his goal of exposing the city of Gulf Shores and its unfair policies of seizing private property, Arthur didn't really know much about Nicholas. He remembered him coming to the gym when his uncle was still alive, but other than that, he couldn't recall anything else about him.

"I'm not doing this just for the money," Arthur protested. "I am also trying to expose a corrupt legal system which has siphoned off land and profits from unsuspecting private citizens for years. That's my real cause, and to honor the memory of your uncle." To be honest, Nicholas could care less about his uncle's legacy or the honor of his memory, but if there were dollars to be extracted from the city of Gulf Shores, Nicholas was up for whatever it took to make that happen. However, he had to appear to be sympathetic to Arthur's cause.

"I agree totally with your cause, Arthur. What can I do to help?" Arthur thought for a moment and then challenged Nicholas.

"This may get messy, and some people may get hurt with what I am planning, so are you up for that kind of thing?" Arthur wanted to make sure that Nicholas was not going to get cold feet and run to the authorities if things got tough.

"I'm in for the duration," he said, offering his hand as a verbal contract. Arthur shook his hand and told him to meet him at the Hangout at 5:00 PM that afternoon to make plans for their big assault on the city.

* * *

Arthur wasn't sure how much he could trust his new friend with, but it was nice to have a co-

conspirator working against the city of Gulf Shores. So far, they had totally ignored Arthur's demands, and they would pay dearly for that reaction before he was finished with them. The next thing he would do is make a monetary demand which he knew the city wouldn't even consider paying, thereby justifying his next steps of violence against the citizens of Gulf Shores. His newest note in the personal ads section of the *Islander* read:

I have considered the damage the city of Gulf Shores has done to the families of Baldwin County and my demands are that they pay $20 million dollars in unmarked $100 bill denomination and place the money in a gym bag. The bag is to be left at the Hangout parking lot, in the men's rooms at precisely 5:00 PM today. If these demands are not met, there could be explosive results.

Unknown to Arthur, Nicholas had seen the article in the Islander and was thrilled to see him begin to demand real restitution for Nicholas' uncle's property loss. Whether or not the city brought $20 million or one million dollars to the Hangout, they would be rich! Nicholas had decided that most of the money delivered for payment was morally his, and he would take it all and run when he got the opportunity. Now, he just had to pay it cool until things developed the way they had planned them.

* * *

"Jonathan, did you see the latest threat that Arthur Murry has made in the *Islander*?" Maggie asked.

"No, what was it?"

"He states that if the city of Gulf Shores doesn't show up with a gym bag with $20 million dollars by 5:00 PM today at the Hangout, there will be *explosive* results."

"Given the fact that he appears to have all the makings of an explosive device, I think we need to take this threat seriously. Let's go see CPT Phillips and see how he wants to handle things. This investigation has moved from threats to possible actions beyond our legal authority, and the chief will have to decide how to move forward from here." Maggie agreed, and they took Jo-Ellen with them as they headed down to the basement and Maggie's Crown Vic. They were burning up the asphalt on Highway 59 North in Maggie's black monster machine, and they got to the police chief's office in five minutes flat. As usual, Maggie parked out front in one of the "*Reserved for police vehicle*" spots. No one challenged her. They walked directly into the chief's office, closed the door behind themselves, and began their discussion with no appointment or invitation to sit down.

"Obviously, there must be something amiss for you to come into my office uninvited," CPT Phillips said. He appeared a little upset that proper protocol was not being followed, but he quickly got over this feeling when Jonathan showed him the article in the *Islander* and told him what Maria had discovered about Arthur Murry.

"What do you propose we do about this Arthur Murry? I can tell you right now that we don't have $20 million, nor would we pay a blackmailer that kind of money if we *did* have it. This man is a home-grown terrorist, and we don't negotiate with terrorists." Jonathan knew that would be the first reaction the chief would have after hearing the news, but they had to come up with some way to appease the potential bomber.

"I suggest that you have some officers appear at the Hangout and take this guy into custody. Maybe we can get him to tell us where he plans to detonate his bomb, assuming he really has constructed one."

"I want all three of you to raise your right hands," CPT Phillips said. Jonathan and Maggie knew what was coming, but Jo-Ellen was clueless. She raised her hand as instructed, and he swore them all in as Special Deputies for the city of Gulf Shores. Nothing else really had to be said by the police chief to the three detectives. They all had licenses to carry firearms, and with the swearing in ceremony they had just experienced, they were now official city marshals for the city of Gulf Shores.

"I'm assuming you would like for us to bring this perp in so you can question him?"

"Dead or alive is fine with me," Phillips said, and he went back to work on the papers on his desk. Jonathan, Maggie, and Jo-Ellen let themselves out of the office, got into the Crown Vic, and they roared off back to the M&J offices. Once they arrived, they saw that Maria had left the library and was again sitting at her desk in the office.

"This is a nice surprise," Jo-Ellen said to Maria. "I thought you'd still be combing over the Internet for clues to what our perp may be planning."

"I think I know," she said solemnly. "I think he'll either attack a bridge or a high-rise building."

"Does that put this building on alert for a possible incident?" Jonathan asked.

"I don't think so," Maria said. "We just have too much security and CCTV cameras in place for him to even plant the device, much less get away with the crime undetected. No, he'll try a much softer target. By the way, where have you three been?"

"We just left the police department and are now official deputies of the city of Gulf Shores," Jo-Ellen said, showing Maria their new badges, which were issued to them when they were sworn in.

"What does that mean?"

"According to CPT Phillips, he wants us to bring him Arthur Murry, dead or alive!" Jo-Ellen said.

"Isn't that a bit radical? I mean, we haven't even really tied him to any crime so far with forensic evidence. Is that a little bit like 'You're guilty until you're proven innocent?' Does he have the authority to issue such a command?"

"It's a moot point, Maria," Jonathan said. "We're not going to go gunning for Arthur Murry. However, if we do get in an altercation with him, I imagine we will shoot first and ask questions later."

"Getting back to the possible targets for a bomber with a limited explosive device, I have listed those soft targets specifically which might be most attractive to him if he really is planning to do something radical."

"Do you have you a list for us?" Maggie asked. Maria handed each of them a list with several buildings' addresses highlighted, and with a number from one to ten to the left of the building's name.

"What do the numbers indicate?" Jonathan asked.

"Those are priority targets which I think he might attack, based upon my research. While there's no specific order in which he might choose to attack, the first few would give him much more visibility than some of the others." On the list, close to the top of the page, were the Intercoastal

Bridge, the U.S. Post Office, Gulf Shores City Hall, the bridge separating Orange Beach from the state of Florida, and the dock at Ft. Morgan. There were also several high-rise condominiums and apartments, as well as the South Baldwin County Medical Center.

"I guess it would be pretty simple to put surveillance teams at each of these locations just in case you're correct in your assumption," Jonathan said. "I noticed our particular condo was not listed, even thought our property is one of the main pieces of land the city had seized in the past."

"The security here is simply too high, unless he decides to make this a suicide bombing. If that's the case, there's little anyone can do to stop such a diabolical attack."

"I'll notify the captain about our best guess where the bomber might strike and see if he wants to put special patrols on those locations until the perp is located and off the street," Jonathan said. The chief was notified, he said he'd increase the number of patrols available for those particular areas, and everyone was holding their collective breath hoping that nothing terrible was going to happen.

Chapter 17
All Bets are Off

As the specific time for the threat to be carried out by Arthur Murry and his new prodigy, Nickolas Douglas, began to get nearer, Arthur made a statement to his comrade in arms that he had decided to call the whole thing off. It was futile to expect someone with such low morals to do the right thing. Arthur had made a perfectly good explosive device which could take down a small building, or perhaps it could dislodge a large bridge support from its base. So, Nicholas wasn't the one getting cold feet, it was Arthur. Nicholas couldn't believe what he was hearing from this radical home-grown terrorist. If Arthur gave up now Nicholas would never see a penny of the money that they had hoped to get from the city for the immoral seizure of Leon Douglas' land.

"You can't do that, Arthur," Nicholas protested. The two men were sitting in the Hangout, having a beer and a burger, and the clock on the wall read 4:30 PM, only thirty minutes from the time when the money was due to be delivered. "Everything is set up, and I truly believe that they will give us some money if we just remain patient. They won't fork over $20 million, but we may get several hundred thousand dollars, and that would be a nice start. We may have to blow up a building or two to make them see that we mean business, but you have enough material for several bombs." Arthur looked at Nicholas with a defeated expression on his face and reiterated that all of the fight had gone out of him, and now he only wanted things to return to normal. He might have to serve some time for the deeds which were already done, but if he threw himself on the mercy of the court, the judge might go easy on him. Nicholas knew he was running out of time as the clock on the wall showed 4:45 PM.

"Let's go to the men's room and discuss this, Arthur," Nicholas said. Reluctantly, Arthur agreed. They had no more walked into the door of the men's room when Arthur felt a very sharp instrument pierce his chest. He had been stabbed in the heart by Nicholas Douglas. Arthur looked down to his chest, red blood was spurting out like liquid from a hot soda bottle, and suddenly Arthur began to sink to the floor. By the time his body had settled down to the floor of the bathroom, he was dead. Nicholas figured he must have struck the main aorta or another major artery for Arthur to die so quickly. Looking at the collapsed corpse of what had once been Arthur Murry, Nicholas thought to himself that it was going to come to this eventually. Nicholas was not going to share whatever money they got from their scheme to bribe the city with a nobody like Arthur Murry! However, now Nicholas had a decision to make, and he had to make it quickly. They were in the public bathroom at the Hangout, and it was at 5:00 PM in the afternoon. There were people everywhere, and there was really no way to efficiently dispose of the body. So, Nicholas wiped his fingerprints off of the blade he had used to end Arthur's life, and he just left the body where it lay on the urine-stained concrete floor. After all, Nicholas thought to himself, Arthur's dead. He didn't have the ability to care at this point.

Nicholas knew that the drop off of the money was probably a moot point for now, what with Arthur's body lying openly on the floor of the restaurant bathroom for all to see. It would only be a few minutes before this news would be spread all over Gulf Shores and the public beach area. Nicholas now had to regroup, create another plausible threat, and collect enough money to escape this crime scene, as well as the entire state of Alabama.

What Nicholas needed most of all was a plan, and one which could be executed almost at once. Arthur had made two bombs, and the detonation of them was a very simple process. Nicholas would blow up something, causing as little collateral damage as was possible, and then renew his threat to destroy something very valuable in a highly populated area with his next bomb. That should get everyone's attention. He also knew that small cities didn't keep millions of dollars of currency lying around for emergencies. Nicholas would reduce his demand from multiple millions of dollars to $100,000. He knew any city could come up with that kind of money almost immediately. Arthur never really expected the city of Gulf Shores to pay a ransom at all, but Nicholas had a different approach to his demands. He would settle for a lot smaller amount of money, but he wanted it quickly and was prepared to kill hundreds of innocent people, if necessary. Arthur had told him the whole story about M&J Investigations, the financing help that the company had provided for the completion of the Crown Victoria Condominiums, and the complicity the city of Gulf Shores had with the entire process. Someone would pay Nicholas or people would die, and they would die soon!

* * *

Maria was working on completing the profile on Arthur Murry when the office phone rang, and she recognized that it was from the Gulf Shores Police Department.

"May I help you?" she asked politely.

"Is this Maria Garcia?" the voice asked.

"It is. Who is calling?"

"This is CPT Lawrence Phillips of the Gulf Shores Police Department. Is Jonathan or Maggie there?"

"Just a moment, Chief," she said. Maria went to the balcony where Jonathan, Maggie, and Jo-Ellen were sipping on iced tea and rocking in the oversized rocking chairs. They had been discussing how to move forward with the detection and capture of Arthur Murry. "Jonathan, you or Maggie need to pick up the office phone extension on the balcony. CPT Phillips needs to speak to one or both of you." Jonathan and Maggie had spoken briefly about their knowledge that Arthur was threatening to use explosives in his next attack, but they didn't have any real strategy to discover how to find him before an attack or when it might happen.

"Captain, I'm going to put you on speaker so everyone can hear our conversation. What's happening?"

"Jonathan, I have some good news and some very bad news," he said.

"Okay," Jonathan said. "Give us the good news first."

"Arthur Murry is dead. He was discovered by a patron at the Hangout just a few minutes ago. There was no note, or anything attached to his corpse, and it appears that the murder weapon had been wiped clean of any fingerprints of his attacker."

"So, what's the bad news?"

"We just received an anonymous telephone call to watch the news at 6:00 PM. There's going to be an explosion. Evidently, Arthur had someone working with him, and that person is the one who murdered Arthur. He says Arthur made two fertilizer bombs, and this guy is going to blow something up to show us that he is not lying. He said the next one will kill many people if we don't agree to his demands."

"And what are his demands?"

"He calls himself the Avenger, and if we don't deliver $100,000 in cash to him within an hour of his demanding it, he will detonate the second bomb."

"Did he sound credible?"

"Well, the demand for money went from $20 million to $100K, so I think he means business. I can't think of a way to prevent the first explosion, so let's just hope he doesn't hurt or kill a lot of innocent people trying to prove to us that he actually has the capacity to explode a second bomb."

"What do you want us to do?"

"There's no way the city of Gulf Shores can come up with $100K quickly. I hate the idea of surrendering to a terrorist, but what else can we do? Can you secure those kinds of funds until we can decide how to justify paying it back? I know it's a lot to ask, but I don't know what else we can do." Jonathan didn't answer for a moment, but when he did his answer surprised the chief.

"Do you really want to pay this terrorist, or just catch him?"

"You must know something that I don't, because I didn't know we had the option to catch him. When did that choice become available to us?" the captain asked.

"As soon as he started making demands that are reasonable."

"And you think paying $100,000 ransom is reasonable?"

"I never said that Captain. I said as soon as he asked for a reasonable amount of money to call off the carnage. Arthur was asking for more money than was reasonable, and that tells me that he had no intention of stopping his rampage because of the money. What I don't understand is this new guy and how he became involved in Arthur's plans and plot to punish the city of Gulf Shores. Once I figure that fact out, we will have a pretty good shot at learning the identity of the new threat to the city."

"What do you think the murder of Arthur means in all of this craziness? Why kill your partner in crime?"

"Jealousy, money, anger, and a few dozen other reasons come to mind, but we may never know why our current outlaw decided to part ways with Arthur Murry."

"You and your staff are excellent detectives. Does anyone have an idea why this new guy has done what he's done and is he capable of setting off an explosive device just to get our attention?" The phone line was silent for few moments until Jo-Ellen spoke.

"If we as detectives really understood the mind of these people, we would be as crazy as they are! However, I'm just guessing, but it's possible that Arthur had a change of heart and decided that he had done enough to satisfy whatever need he had to try and embarrass the city of Gulf Shores for their questionable land-grab practices. Legal or not, I doubt anyone in their right mind would agree with any government office condemning a person's property, selling it at auction, and making millions of dollars in profits from such a despicable act. However, the solution is to expose the crooked politicians, incarcerate them, have them pay huge financial fines to restore the funds that they literally stole from the original landowners, and handle things legally. We all know that crooks don't work through legal channels, so revenge becomes a tool in the hands of someone like Arthur Murry. I would guess that Arthur's accomplice thought that Arthur was going to abandon the money aspect of the threat to the city, and he wasn't going to let that happen. Knowing that the city could never come up with millions and millions of dollars, the perp used pretty sound logic asking for a greatly reduced sum of money to go away and not kill anyone else. That would be my guess." No one else on the phone call spoke, and the captain finally said that her guess was as good as anything else he had going, so he wanted them to pursue the new perp as if what Jo-Ellen described were the actual facts of what happened.

"How can we narrow down this new guy's probable attack area, and when do you expect him to act?"

"I doubt he has changed the targets which Arthur Murry had originally chosen, and I imagine we'll hear from him very soon as he demonstrates his ability to carry out the more dangerous threat," Maggie said. Just then the captain told them that he had to go, but he would call them back soon.

"What do you think that abruptness was all about?" Jonathan asked.

"Maybe the original threat of a 'demonstration' has taken place and the captain just heard about it. Maria, turn on the police scanner on the desk and let's listen to the chatter to see if we can decide if something has happened," Maggie said. Maria turned on the scanner, turned up the volume so everyone could hear it, and they listened to the dispatcher call more and more officers to a particular location.

"Any officer in the vicinity of the small bridge on Highway 59 just north of the Gulf Shores beach area please respond to a 10-39, 10-50, and a 10-89." Several patrol cars acknowledged the requests and headed toward the bridge in question.

"What's a 10-39,10-50, and 10-89?" Maria asked. "I'm familiar with 10-4 and 10-7, but I've never heard these codes before." Jo-Ellen answered Maria in a memorized tone, as if she used those codes all the time.

"A 10-39 is authorization to use one's siren and flashing lights. A 10-50 is the code for an accident with fatalities. Usually, the respondent to this type of call is an ambulance or the fire department. And a 10-89 is the code for a bomb threat. It sounds like our perp's first bomb, the signal that he really does have the capacity to act in a more destructive manner, has detonated and he's begun his countdown to the larger, more dangerous explosion which he just threatened to carry out when he called the police department."

"What can we do to stop this maniac?" Maria asked.

"Maria, look again at all the personal information you found on the previous owner of the property where the Crown Victoria Condominiums were built," Jonathan said. "I think we found Arthur Murry from that information. Maybe there's other information naming the next of kin to the victim who died in the fire at the old warehouse." Maria quickly pulled up all the electronic files on the old case which had been disputed by Arthur Murry over the past few years.

"The victim's name was Leon Douglas, he was married and had two small children when he died, and there's mention of a Nicholas Douglas as a nephew, but doesn't live locally."

"That's the best lead we have, so let's run with it," Maggie said. "Jo-Ellen, call the airlines, Amtrak, and the bus lines and see if anyone named Nicholas Douglas, or a similar name, booked travel to Gulf Shores in the past week or so. Maria, check with all the local motels and hotels and see if they have him as a registered guest. Jonathan and I will get in my Crown Vic, and we will be patrolling the Gulf Shores public beach area until we hear something from you two. We need to find this guy before he kills a bunch of innocent people."

As Jonathan and Maggie were in the elevator preparing to take her car to the beach and other public area to look for signs of a possible attack, Jonathan's phone rang. It was CPT Phillips again.

"Sorry I had to hang up so quickly a few minutes ago, but we had an emergency."

"The bridge?" Maggie asked.

"How did you two hear about the bridge?"

"We have a first-class police scanner, Chief," Jonathan said. "We heard the 10-50 and 10-89 codes. Was someone injured in the blast?"

"Unfortunately, a couple on vacation from Ashburn, Alabama, were killed when their car exploded along with the bridge just before you get to the Original Oyster House Boardwalk. No other structures were damaged, but the bridge will be out for a few days until we can get it repaired, which means people will have to go to Orange Beach on Highway 135 and come back west on the beach highway to get to the public beach areas of Gulf Shores. I'm assuming you two are on that side of the creek."

"That is correct. I think we may have caught a break in the case."

"Just tell me how you plan to keep this nut from blowing up a major bridge or a high-rise building and threatening to kill many more innocent lives."

"We've traced a distant relative of the owner of the warehouse who died in the fire which gutted the old building, making the land available for condemning and resale to buyers on the county courthouse steps."

"I'm not following your logic. How does that help us right now?"

"We think that Arthur Murry must have had a partner who double-crossed him, murdered him at the Hangout, and changed Arthur's plans somewhat to try and get a reasonable amount of cash and then split town. And get this. His name is Nicholas Douglas, the nephew of the original owner of the property the city seized from the family of the deceased."

"What are the odds he is our man?" the captain asked. "And, assuming your suspicions are correct, how do find if he is in town?"

"We're working on that right now, but I can tell you if he took public transportation of any kind, or if he checked into a local hotel or motel, we'll find him," Jonathan said. "When was the deadline he gave you when he called back and made the second bomb threat?"

"He wants the money in small, unmarked bills, delivered to the Hangout, placed in a particular garbage can, and no police presence, by 4:00 PM tomorrow afternoon. Which gives us about eighteen hours until we have a major catastrophe on our hands."

"A lot can happen in eighteen hours, Captain. We'll keep you informed if we discover anything worth mentioning. Keep the faith," Maggie said as cheerfully as she could muster. As soon as she hung up, Jonathan's phone rang, and he recognized Jo-Ellen's cell number.

"Tell me you've found our perp," Jonathan said as he put his phone on speaker.

"Here's what we know. An N. Douglas arrived in Gulf Shores yesterday on a Greyhound Bus from Boston, Massachusetts. He checked into the Best Western Inn at the Gulf Shores Beach in room 506. According to the girl on the desk, the tenant in that room called down to ask where he could order food to be delivered to his room."

"When was that call made?" Maggie asked.

"Less than an hour ago, and the clerk said that someone delivered a pizza to his room just a few minutes ago. He's probably up there eating his dinner and unaware that we are onto him."

"Okay. Jonathan and I are near the Hangout, but since our offices are so close to the Best Western Inn, why don't you put your vest on, arm yourself to the teeth, and meet us in the lobby of the hotel in ten minutes. We want to surprise him, but we don't want anyone else in a crossfire if he is armed."

"Got it! Maybe I will get to shoot the bastard!"

"Just wait in the lobby for us and don't make a move until we get there. We will work out a strategy before we go up to his room." Jo-Ellen agreed, began putting on her vest and weapon, and that naturally drew attention from Maria.

"What's happening? Are you going to try to bring him in?"

"Maria don't worry. Jonathan, Maggie, and I have done this a number of times before. We want to use the element of surprise and catch the perp in his room and subdue him before he can harm anyone else."

"Please promise me you'll be careful," she cautioned.

"I promise that I will. What I want you to do is do an in-depth background search on Nicholas Douglas and let me know what you find."

"What am I looking for?"

"I don't know but look for anything that is out of the ordinary. You should text me, not call me, when you have anything that may help us when we confront this guy." Maria agreed, Jo-Ellen kissed her on the head, and Jo-Ellen headed for the elevator.

Chapter 18
Playing the Long Game

Jo-Ellen, Maggie, and Jonathan all arrived in the lobby of the Best Western Inn at the same time. The time was 10:00 PM, and the lobby was quiet and only the desk clerk was on duty. They quickly explained the situation, told her that they wanted her to pull the fire alarm, notify all guests that there had been a suspected fire in one of the rooms, and the entire hotel must be evacuated as soon as possible. The clerk's name was Ellie Brown, she was twenty-three years old, and she was terrified. She was staring at the detectives' personal firearms, bulletproof vests, and other paraphernalia which they had hanging from their utility belts.

"What do you want me to do?" Ellie said, the words catching in her throat.

"First, Ellie, take a deep breath," Jonathan told her. He smiled at her and repeated the fire drill request. "We believe that there is a very dangerous person in room 506, and we want to try and subdue him without anyone else getting hurt. Once you pull the alarm, notify all the residents by turning on the fires alarm, you may leave out the front door. We will handle things from there. How many rooms are rented tonight?'

"Since this is a weeknight, and not in the middle of the tourist season, there are few rooms occupied. We were full for the Gulf Shores

Shrimp Festival all last week, but most of those people checked out yesterday."

"Are there any other exits, other than the elevators and the stairwells on either end of the building?" Jo-Ellen asked.

"Not that I know of, but I've only been here a few weeks."

"That's okay. Give us three minutes and then set off the fire alarm," Maggie said. Ellie nodded her head in agreement, the three detectives split up, with Jonathan taking the near stairs, Jo-Ellen the far stairs, and Maggie pulled her Glock and entered the elevator. They were all three waiting outside room 506 when the fire alarm began to wail. Inside the concrete walls of the high-rise, it sounded much louder than they had expected. They waited sixty seconds for everyone to clear the floor, saw no one, and used the electronic door key to enter Nicholas Douglas' room. Maggie was the first through the door.

"Nicholas Douglas, come out with your hands up!" she shouted as she flipped on the room lights, checked the bathroom, and saw that the room was unoccupied. "How did he get by us?" Maggie asked. She went out on the balcony, saw a sheet tied to the balcony railing, and pointed it out to Jonathan and Jo-Ellen.

"Jo-Ellen, go back down the staircase you used to get up here, I'll go back down mine, and Maggie can search the rooms, one by one, until we find him," Jonathan said. Maggie had already pulled her Glock, so she proceeded to check every room on the fifth floor to no avail. How could he just disappear?

“I see him,” Jo-Ellen shouted from the ground floor. “He used the laundry chute to get to the first floor. He’s carrying something in his arms, and he’s headed to the Pink Pony Pub.”

“Follow him, Jo-Ellen, and don’t lose him. We’ll corner him somewhere and end this nightmare,” Jonathan said. Jo-Ellen shouted that she would do just that, and then she was gone. Maggie and Jonathan went by the front desk, told the clerk that everything was fine now, and that she could start let people return to their rooms. Ellie was as white as a sheet. Now, they had to find Jo-Ellen and the perp, disarm him of his explosive device, and end this craziness. Jonathan’s phone lit up, but it didn’t ring. He had a text message from Jo-Ellen saying that the perp had fled from the hotel to the beach, ran up the ramp of the Pink Pony Pub, and was inside. She had not tried to enter, and she didn’t know if he was holding any hostages or not.

“Our perp is in the Pink Pony Pub, and Jo-Ellen is watching from outside. She didn’t want to enter and spook him. Let’s get over there and help her,” Jonathan said quietly. They moved stealthily, and it only took a few minutes for them to reach the Pink Pony Pub on foot. They saw Jo-Ellen standing in the shadows, quietly approached her, and the three of them began to develop a strategy to get to the perp without causing injury to the people in the pub. The Pink Pony Pub was a favorite night spot on the beach, and during the seasonal times it was usually packed with patrons until it closed around 11:00 PM nightly. Fortunately, there were only a few cars outside in the parking area, and there were no patrons on the deck overlooking the Gulf of Mexico.

"Maggie, what do you think we should do?" Jonathan asked.

"This has really been your gig from the beginning, Jonathan. I think you should make the call."

"Okay. This is what we'll do. Maggie and I will split up, I'll watch the rear of the pub, Maggie will watch the front where the deck is located. Jo-Ellen, you stay here and guard against the perp from escaping down the ramp to the parking lot. I also think it's time to call in the calvary." Jonathan picked up his phone, dialed CPT Phillips at the police precinct, filled him in on what had happened, and suggested that he send a squad of cars, but to send them 10-40, with no lights or sirens. Jonathan didn't want to spook the perp unnecessarily if he could prevent it. The captain was more than happy to fulfill Jonathan's request, and in a matter of ten minutes or less there were several uniformed police personnel surrounding the Pink Pony Pub. As soon as everyone was in place, Jonathan texted Jo-Ellen and Maggie and they decided to meet at the location where Jo-Ellen was standing in the shadows.

"Now what do you suggest, Jonathan?" Maggie asked. She really had no idea how they were going to avoid the loss of life with this perp in a no-win situation, and many times such cases ended with "death by cop," and nobody wanted that to happen. Surprisingly, Jo-Ellen spoke up, and it gave Jonathan an idea.

"I got a text from Maria. She said all she could really find out about Nicholas Douglas was that he was an avowed narcissist. He only thought about himself and the things that touched him. Everything else was expendable, but he valued his own life too much to put it in harm's way. How can that help us in this situation?" Jonathan thought for a moment and made a suggestion which gave both Jo-Ellen and Maggie chills.

"You really would tell him that?" Jo-Ellen asked. Jonathan had studied psychology between his college graduation and entering Harvard Law School. If any of the three of them had any experience or expertise reading the psychic minds of perps, it was Jonathan. Narcissism was not the focus of his study, but he knew enough about such people that it gave him the confidence to dare Nicholas to blow himself up with the patrons of the Pink Pony Pub.

"Jo-Ellen, I agree with you that tempting the perp to blow himself up is a bit out of the range of how we might handle a terrorist situation in most cases, but I also have confidence that Jonathan probably knows best in this case. If we go in blasting our weapons, someone's probably going to die who shouldn't. I'd rather not have any collateral damage that can be avoided, and this may be the best chance we have for that."

"Here's how we set things up. We make sure CPT Phillips' men don't get trigger-happy and rush in and destroy our plan. I will go into the pub unarmed, offer myself as Nicholas' hostage, and encourage him to let the other people in the pub go free. Assuming he is willing to do that, I will have a serious discussion with him about ending his life. I think he will crumble like an old piece of cornbread when he's faced with the reality that he may die."

"And you're willing to do that?" Jo-Ellen asked.

"Do you have a better idea?" he asked.

"No, but that's risky."

"It's risky, but I'm playing the long game here."

"What do you mean?"

"The odds of someone taking their own life with others is greatest when the perp thinks there is nothing to live for. Why not just end it all, and take as many other people with him when he dies? However, we're not dealing with a depressed loser here. We're dealing with a pretty intelligent perp who believes his continued existence on this planet is necessary for humanity itself. I think he's scared we will shoot him, not that he will kill himself and all of us with him with a homemade bomb. Ask the captain to have the bomb-squad standing by as well."

Maggie relayed Jonathan's message to the captain, he relayed it to his people, and everyone waited for Jonathan to walk up the ramp into the Pink Pony Pub.

"Do you want to wear this padded suit?" one of the bomb experts asked Jonathan as he took his Glock and handed it to Maggie.

"No, because if he sets that bomb off, it won't keep me from being blown up with everything around me. I want this perp to see how cool and calm I am under pressure."

"But are you that cool?" Maggie asked.

"Cool enough. Let's do this," he said, and he began walking up the ramp.

* * *

As Jonathan walked into the Pink Pony Pub main dining room, he saw three people sitting at a table, with a separate person sitting behind them on a stool, holding what appeared to be a large briefcase. There were no other people in the pub, and it looked like only the manager, a waitress, and one customer were being detained by the perp.

"Don't come any closer or I'll set this bomb off and blow us all up," Nicholas said. Jonathan noticed that Nicholas was covered in sweat, and it wasn't hot or humid in the pub.

"Nicholas, why don't you let those three people go, and you and I can talk this thing out between just the two of us," Jonathan said.

"I'll set this thing off! Don't test me," he said.

"We know you're not going to blow us up, Nicholas. You're too important a person for that to happen at your own hands. Right?" Nicholas thought for a moment and nodded affirmatively.

"I messed things up, didn't I?" and he looked helplessly at Jonathan.

"There's nothing you've done that can't be fixed, but first, you need to let these three innocent people go. You can keep me as a hostage. You and I can talk things out between us. See, I don't have a weapon. It'll just be you and me talking. How about it?"

"What if I say no?" Nicholas asked.

"Well, then all those policemen outside may come bursting into the pub and shoot you dead. You wouldn't want that to happen, would you?"

"Yeah, but they might shoot you as well," he said.

"That's true, but you're more important than me. Right? I'm expendable, but you're not. There's only one of you. Think about it. You don't want to gamble that they might end your life, do you?"

"I guess not. Okay, they can go, but you have to stay." Jonathan walked calmly to the door, opened it for the three hostages, and they quickly moved outside and away from the building. Jonathan, true to his word, came back inside and sat by Nicholas.

"I know you didn't mean to hurt those people who died when the bridge was destroyed, but you had to do it. Right? That's part of being superior to other people. You see things that they cannot see or understand. Was that why Arthur Murry had to die? Was he not capable of seeing the big picture?"

"I tried to tell him, but he wouldn't listen, so I had to take control. He should have listened to me. I would have given him some of the money we were going to get from the city of Gulf Shores, but he got cold feet and I had to take over. You can see my point, can't you?"

"I think enough people have been hurt, don't you? You need to give me that device so I can dispose of it, and you won't get hurt by it. It could explode and either maim you or kill you. That wouldn't be right, would it?" Nicholas thought again and nodded affirmatively. He pushed the box to Jonathan. Jonathan picked it up carefully, walked it to the door, motioned for the bomb squad to come retrieve the package, and once they had it, Jonathan went back inside the pub. No other sounds came from the pub for at least ten minutes, and then the door opened, and the two men exited the Pink Pony Pub as if they had been friends for life.

Epilogue

What causes some people to act out and create havoc, while other people faced with similar situations and conditions adjust and continue to live peaceably in civilized society? How can two people see the same data, conditions, and life around them and react so differently? Morality is a factor, and so is proper upbringing and teachings learned at the feet of our parents and guardians. Why do some people grow up to be nice, considerate souls who do for others, have empathy for their neighbors, and are generally considered peacemakers? While others seem to have been born under a black cloud, never having things work out for themselves, and having to prove to the world that they are worthy of the same love and consideration everyone else.

Leon Davis was one of the good guys. He gave back to his community and to all those who were in need of consideration, yet he was accidentally murdered by whoever set the fire which burned down his gym and took his life in the process. Why does God let things like that happen? Why not bring bad things upon the drug dealer, the murderers, rapists, and those who go through life stealing the very life blood from those innocents like Leon Davis? It doesn't seem fair.

And then there are people like Arthur Murry. A man who cared about his neighbor, his friend Leon Douglas, and only wanted justice for him and his family when he was brutally murdered by an arsonist, his estate stolen by the local government, and no one caring to do anything about it. Arthur had pledged to his departed friend that he, Arthur, would avenge his death, reclaim the assets stolen from his family and taken by the government, even if it caused him to lose his own life. It was a self-fulfilling prophesy.

Jonathan, Maggie, and Jo-Ellen had worked some unusual cases since they set up the M&J Investigation Agency, but in the end, this case proved to be very frustrating for all of them. Yes, they solved the mystery of the perp who wanted revenge from the city of Gulf Shores, but did their investigation really change things? Only time would tell.

www.ingramcontent.com/pod-product-compliance
Lightning Source LLC
LaVergne TN
LVHW041157150826
845673LV00001B/194

* 9 7 9 8 8 0 1 4 2 1 4 8 3 *